Gossips
of Reality

ABOO

Gossips of Reality

PARTRIDGE

A Penguin Random House Company

ISBN: Hardcover   978-1-4828-1418-7
               Softcover   978-1-4828-1417-0
               Ebook   978-1-4828-1419-4

To order additional copies of this book, contact
Partridge India
000 800 10062 62
www.partridgepublishing.com/india
orders.india@partridgepublishing.com

ACKNOWLEDGEMENT

To all the kind souls that has touched my life—
Thank you!

Here I am today, somewhere in my life; betrayed by my own thoughts, I find myself in a world unknown.

The whole universe in me is on a roller-coaster ride, nothing around me makes sense and yet everything in it is in its perfect existence.

Is this a dream . . . ?

If it is, I want to wake up. I have had too much fun!

Night was headed towards the end of a battle with the morning light; slowly, it was being torn apart. The day was about to begin, but the night was in no mood to give away; and it was holding back—just as much as it could—to cast its final shadows. It looked like a never-ending saga.

Taking advantage of the situation, my lazy little soul was quick to drag me into a dialogue with my mind and convince it that a little extra sleep would harm nobody. I stretched out to check for the time; it was four in the morning. Perfect! I could slip in some extra hours of snooze before I started a long, mundane routine.

As I was struggling to get myself back to sleep, my thoughts started to wander like a travelling soul. Instantly I was transported to a different universe, the one that I was yet to be introduced to.

Somehow there was a bizarre understanding and yet everything seemed familiar in this world. I found myself in a state where I was neither asleep nor awake. I was somewhere—I know for sure. I could feel it . . . But where had I been? That would be the question, the question that would haunt me for days to come.

The early birds announced their arrival by tearing up the silence with their morning songs. Then it was the roosters' turn—of course. They suddenly decided to join in the harmony. *It must have been more of a compulsion for the roosters to announce the arrival of the day, as for the birds, they sounded genuinely happy with the departure of darkness.*

As I slowly gained my consciousness and gazed at the clock that was hanging on the wall opposite to my bed, the clock struck six. It was exactly two hours since the last memory I could recollect.

My first thought of that day . . . if I recollect it correctly, was—where am I?

This is not a place where I last went to sleep. There is something about this place that is different? Even though every single piece of furniture, the colour on the wall, the carpet, and every single curtain look the same, something inside me tells me it is not.

I slowly got up from the bed and made my way towards the bathroom. It was a creepy silence that suddenly entered my head, and it started to grow quiet, more and more in its intensity.

It grew until the pain of it, no longer could I tolerate. I screamed my heart out. In a moment of madness, I threw a vase towards the mirror, which instantly gave itself away and was lying martyred on the floor.

The silence was gone.

I could hear a shrilling voice calling curses as if it was a favourite song of hers. I had got used to those chants long time ago, and sometimes I could hear her scream for hours at a stretch. It wouldn't bother me.

I reckon I got acquainted to the rhythms of her mood swings and had found my escape by starting to like it.

Yeah, funny the way it is, huh? It's true. This way no one got hurt.

Oh! By the way, that's Nadja, with her ever hateful words and yet none of them intended to hurt anyone. 'Remember that.'

We shared a two-bedroom apartment on the sixteenth floor of the Residency Towers next to a beautiful lake in the garden city of India. When I look back in memories, I think it must have been my newfound freedom then of not relying any more on the monthly budget duly sanctioned by Sir Major that gave me the required boost to take up this place as my home.

How humble of me then to think I had enough in me and was always born ready to be something destined for.

What? Yeah, that was the big question to be asked.

Or was it the evening sunset that stole my heart and made me stay here? Whatever it was, at that point of my life, I knew there was no other place I would call a home.

Funny, how some events in your life can forever change the course of the journey ahead! Never knew about it.

Long story on how she ended up sharing an apartment with me. I am sure you must be curious to know; let me keep it simple so you don't lose the story in-between. Here it goes . . .

Nadja Engel—I met her during my days in college. She was an exchange student from Germany, and her story was somewhat unreal and yet inviting to listen. I guess years of her unknown hate towards me had drained her out, and it seemed as if she could continue no more when I met her later in my life.

As for me, I really do not have any reasons why I tolerated her unbearable personality. *Guess I had learnt it early as a kid; never give away yourself to smaller trouble.*

Or, maybe I was not too bothered with what she had to say. Yup! That might be the only reason why I could tolerate her then. True, I never listened to her.

But something about her drew me closer to her; no matter how hard I tried to stay away, we were always crossing our paths, even more often.

When I first met her, I found her name quite unusual and had made use of the new-age search tool to help me understand the meaning of her name better . . .

There it was in bold—*Nadja*—meaning *Hope*.

They've made quite a leap in technology . . .

Something about that name just sat there with me for a while. May be it was the way she pronounced it—'Naid-ya'.

Well, that is not how it was spelt though, but she called her what she called herself.

1

My name is Kabir Gurung, born into an army family. Father, a Gorkha from Darjeeling; and mother, a Punjabi brought up in New Delhi.

They tell me they met in the set of a TV documentary show. And as the story goes . . . She had to interview him on the life of an Indian army officer . . . After a couple of questions, guess what . . . *Love had to happen.*

In olden times of our folks, the only way to prove that your love is eternal was to tie the knot with their beloved. But times for them were not as simple as it may appear to the modern India. The majority in India was against the idea of different community and inter-caste marriages, and the only solution to their togetherness was to elope and get married . . . and so they did.

A new story began. Dad and Mom lawfully wedded and were ready to start up a new life.

They probably would have imagined the family they would have and the story they would write together for generations to talk about. *'Well, they seemed to have forgotten something?'*

I was about to enter their life. Promising everything they wanted to believe and finding the truth for myself, they journey of my life was about to begin . . .

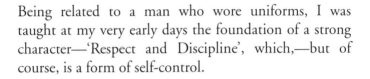

Being related to a man who wore uniforms, I was taught at my very early days the foundation of a strong character—'Respect and Discipline', which,—but of course, is a form of self-control.

Respect, I understood, but discipline is what always troubled me.

How can anyone impose a guideline to someone else's life?

I don't know where this thought came from then . . . Can a three-year-old think such things?

My dad had been promoted as major in the artillery unit of the Indian Army, and so as his duty demanded, he was transferred to the frontiers of the western borders.

I really don't recollect much of which regiment he belonged to, nor his friends, his advises, his jokes, and his stories. I never paid attention to those.

What do I remember?

Life was just ahead in time, round the corner, waiting for me . . . .

I never remembered much about what my parents did. I dwelled in my own universe. I was turning into this question mark which was getting bigger and bigger. I must have been four by then when my dad, who had trained hundreds of officers to be disciplined, gave up hope on me. And a man disappointed, decided that I needed some serious attention.

I was to be sent off to one of the boarding schools.

Hold on! Where was the word boarding coming from?

Thoughts started leaking my mind . . .

You see then, my mom was heavily occupied with the household chores and the kitty parties with the rest of the army officers' wives, and Dad had just grown into a person who required an appointment—just to fit in a moment of his minutes for us.

Boarding seemed fine to me, though deep down, I was scared, scared for my existence.

You see, as a child, you hear stories. The kind in which there are evil. I am sure you must have heard one or seen one for yourself when you were a kid.

Likewise, I had been fed with stories by some of the officers' kids already surviving at some of the renowned boarding schools. They updated me with stories: stories on how one would be shaped right if found deviating from the set moral codes.

Sounded like a place I should have stayed away from. But the curious mind calls itself an explorer ever since I have known him. How was it to be stopped?

It wasn't until I landed there as a boarding student myself that I learnt that there is so much to learn in life, and life itself never stops teaching you, even if the lessons were enough.

My fate was sealed, and it would be in one of the schools in Darjeeling where I was to get enrolled. Mom and Dad went busy putting up the list of renowned schools with boarding facilities up in the hills. Finally, both agreed that an all-boys school in a small hill town of Darjeeling would be the perfect place to help me groom myself into a man—the one that my parents always wanted me to be.

The day arrived when I was finally in front of my new address. I was completely unaware that it would stick around with me for a while. A decade and a tad bit over . . .

Anyways who's to know where you end up learning everything that you can learn about life? Who really knows?

There I was standing in front of a long corridor that walked right into a big reception hall with neatly arranged seats towards the corner of the room. The corridor had been done simple and was coloured with chocolate-brown paints to match the natural colour of the wood that covered the ceilings. Each pillar was neatly complemented by a shining brass vase, and each one of it held a single green stem with a glowing white lily at the end. There was a silence which I cannot explain. Not a living soul made any sound more than their breathing in it.

What is this place? Why is everyone so suddenly different?

I looked around and saw my parents; they both had turned pleading to get me enrolled in this so-called esteemed institution.

I would still like to believe it was only due to the luggage that my parents had brought along that helped me secure the admission in this particular institution. (A big tin box, a mattress set; bucket with a small jug inside, plastic bags with God knows filled with what? Only dad and mom knew what they had managed to place inside it.) It must have given the surety of their intention to the administrators, I was here to stay.

Fr. George Pinto, I believe was the principal then. He looked at me and asked, 'Do you want to study here?'

My answer as a four-year-old was, *'As long as it does not hurt anyone.'* He immediately approved my stay . . .

My dad, Major Viran Gurung, was the most elated that particular day. Finally, his son was studying in a renowned establishment he had only dreamt of, and his list of what it could mean for my future went on . . .

I shall be the son he had always dreamt I would turn out to be; I shall become—sorry I missed to retain his wish list back then.

Dreams, dreams, and dreams all over, and all I wanted to tell him was, 'Dad, be here now. Let me start first and then will see how our dreams fall together. I don't want to dream ahead. I just want to make every memory of my life a dream.'

Just when I was about to start sharing the long running dialogue in my mind and had only uttered the opening statement to my speech, 'Dad . . . ,' my mom, Pariniti Khanna Gurung, made some weird sound and pulled me aside. She somehow knew exactly what I was about to say—she knew that allowing me to share my thought would have had a negative impact to my very own little universe.

I don't know how she did it, but she did it then . . . It made me go quiet and think it was best to say nothing than to be misunderstood.

My parents took me to the dormitory, and after an hour-long straight work, they finally got me settled into my new existence. Dad and Mom were tearful, but they chose not to show their weakness in front of me and pretended they were much braver souls.

They forgot again?

They forgot about the blood which was running inside me. Blood from a dad that was never ready to back out and of a Punjabi mom, the one that was always boiling to explode any given moment.

Guess it was genetics in me, but most were uneducated then to understand the reality to it. If only the majority around were just a little mature and educated, everything would have turned a little different for me.

But stupid that they were then, stupid is what got me here today, that *my story had to be written the way it had to be.*

My introduction to life had me, from a very early age, chasing behind something unknown. Something that I knew was right in front of me, but it always eluded my reality. I reminded myself every single day to focus and find the answers to the questions that kept haunting my memories. I kept reminding myself to take no small cause that would hurt the purpose of my existence in this reality.

I reminded myself that I would not mess around with anyone, and no one messes with me. I was somehow in control of the blood running inside me, I was always the master.

God, I was four and I was thinking all this. Why? I don't know.

Something in me told me then, *'If one stays below the radar, they go by smooth. And for some, no matter how hard they avoid the radar, somehow they still get detected.'*

Sadly, I would fall in the latter one, of course.

I guess it was the genetics in me that got everyone curious. Mostly, strange questions as, 'Is your mom really a Punjabi?' were being shot at me. And as soon as I answered them positive, another rapid fire came through my way.

'And your dad, is he really a Gorkha?' And again, I used to answer them with a definite 'Yes'.

And then another set of questions would follow—'What kind of food do you eat at home?' etc.

I used to get amused by these questions. I would educate them that we used to be a rather normal family. Eating regular foods, just like them.

Any fool could have thought that they were being tested by the crowd to prove their worth of being born with testosterone. Somehow I never thought I was being provoked to stand the trial just for being born a man. I survived gracefully.

First rule of being born a man—you don't show you are scared. That was the first lesson my dad had taught me.

Most of the time, I was being myself. I don't know if any part of me showed that I was not, but I knew I was never.

Funny, people were asking me more about my parents than myself. Maybe it was for the fact that my friends were mostly locals then, and none of them had parents with a different mother tongue. This might have fascinated their thoughts, and they would request me to speak in Punjabi at times. Trust me, I was not bothered about the language then. But I knew a couple of words in Punjabi, and I used to dish it out—just fine.

There used to be laughter in the air, a madness experienced with a few in your life. Those were the friends I met during my stay at the boardings. Almost for over a decade, they were my family. Some coming in and some leaving me behind, they taught me the most precious lesson of my life.

Everything changes in time, so do you. But the focus is not on the change but the picture the changes leave behind. The memories that you build can last more than what your heart can imagine.

During my stay at the boarding, I used my time to observe everything around me. I observed the nature, the animals, the buildings, the sidewalks, and mostly, humans and the human relationships.

Most of my life, I had been busy being what someone else saw of me, but in my new-found life at the school, I was playing no more hide-and-seek.

Again, I was only four, and I already spoke about life, God help me!

Free from the hate of being disciplined, I found my way of learning something new—by breaking it and evaluating the consequences.

Doing analysis on 'cause and impact' and making new theories based on data obtained from the experiments conducted from our newly designed mischief. *Life was a limit unknown.*

I forgot about the world where I came from. The world I had been for so long had been a garden of instruction that had no room to break free.

Here, I was 'free and me'. Not that there were no instructions here for us to follow, but I chose to break them whenever an opportunity presented itself.

I learnt to observe and learn that everything that touches your life has some knowledge to take you further with your journey in time. Do not pass a remark but remember to observe—observe in silence with no thoughts pushing its way.

Friends those days were more of a character to meet. The ones you'll never forget. *Wherever they might be now, hope their souls are safe and sound.*

Story of life, Yeah! That's right . . .

Who you spend your time growing up with, very few of them will be left around. See, back then, we never understood that the story kept on changing. We never knew we shall be meeting people ahead in time, and how they would walk a different path with us and make a new journey together . . . Whatever it may be? Time will come when you will come across a crossroad, and one needs to find the path they need to take ahead. It could be lonely, it could be troublesome, it could be a party, and it could be filled with cheers from the crowd. Anything could be ahead of us in the path that we select from the crossroad; and sometimes we never know which one to take.

Growing up, I never cared about where I stood, but I stood everywhere. School days were filled with folks that had their paintings engraved in the memories of time . . .

Just like those seniors . . .

The good, the bad, the ugly, and the rock star. And the town filled with drama queens and the chocolate heroes writing their fairy tales; the evil conspiring and lurking in the dark—it gave a lot for us to keep ourselves engaged with our own moments then.

A little bit of all had seeped in through us like quick sand that grabbed and took one to a world unknown—only imagination survived here. We rolled the days as it came, being whoever we could be in time then.

I remember there was this guy called Mr Big. Though he looked abnormally large, with his built to be attending any school back then, but that was not why he got christened as 'Mr Big' for. There was some other reason behind his alternate reality.

Legend has it that he was a diehard fan of the band 'Mr Big', and every function held in the school would demand his hit—single, 'Wild World' by Mr Big.

Rumours broadcasted that he was better known as Mr Big in our neighbouring schools too. Such was the legend that no one knew his real name. Mr Big is what he will be remembered, most probably till the day he dies.

I guess you kind of get the idea of individuals surrounding us at that moment, right?

The ones like the uncannily dressed. Seasons of Jeans and Ts; and any dress down intervals—there they were with their checked shirts, buttons opened, and inside, flashing a plain white T, which wrote all over it that they cared less of what others thought. Their pants, of course army smuggled, or . . .

It might have been given to them on charity? Anyway, it used to be neatly tugged inside the long necks of their Dr Martens boots.

Oh yes! The ones with yellow stitches, dark black leather, and a transparent sole to flaunt.

They were the four middle-section gentlemen who sported the same looks and walked their ways together. Their dad or uncles might have been in the army . . .

. . . For a while, thoughts stormed my mind and dragged me to Sir Major. Bingo! He wore the uniforms too; I could have also salvaged something from his outworn outfit and made myself the outfit that made me say—I cared none. But then, there was something else I had to find—it was not the time for me to live in someone else's world.

Those four were to remain in my life for some time before they completed their studies and went pursuing what life demanded of them.

Game over, about time for redemption. God knows what has happened of them, but ever since they left that gate that day, very few have I heard of them. Well, surprisingly, the losses, though, felt heavily were never for too long, there was always someone entering the picture with a new surprise.

Characters they were, what made them.

You see, growing up, the lessons are to be learnt very quickly.

There were numerous learnings that had to be gained, some had to be experienced to talk about, and the most important of all, some lessons never ended and only time could finally teach you what you needed to learn from it.

So I guess, by now, you can pretty much draw up a fair picture of life then.

What I would later learn about life and the reasons for the way it is? Surprise! Surprise!

Lessons that stood as scaffolding had now been removed for the building to shine. The day was nearing when we would have exhausted our stay at the boarding. The only immediate danger was being recalled back at the headquarters by Sir Major. It would quickly send my fate sealing to attend a designated home-driven college. I would be caged in the monotony of Sir Major's discipline to which I shared quite a different relation so far.

In Sir Major's unit, breaking discipline would mean too much at stakes. How do I redeem myself from this? It was the battle that was running forever on my mind, and it did not seem to find an end.

I then heard one of my classmates talking about moving to Delhi to pursue his higher studies.

'What else, there you go, somewhere to go at least.'

I talked my curious mind to give it a shot with Sir Major and convince him on my Delhi migration plan.

The day came when the final goodbyes were being exchanged with the comrades who had spent their entire childhood, being around.

Some of them had been in my life ever since I can recollect, some made their journey in time to that place and had been comrades for a while, and some we met along the way—while growing up.

And then again, I reminded myself—what a man's got to do, he's got to do . . . Move on.

2

My parents were standing on the hallway waiting for me to join them. They were timely, sharing glances with me from behind the crowd which had gathered around to leave their home before and were sharing their final thoughts. I shared my goodbyes with my friends and made my way towards the place where my parents were standing. There was an old green Gypsy waiting for us. Dad made me hop into the second section of the jeep and then he swiftly opened the door in front for Mom. Mom, always the lady, promptly thanked my dad for his generosity.

I can never forget that smile on my dad's face. Took him a while to get where he wanted to reach, to crack his face and crease his mouth to get that funny shape that one calls smile. But it was there, finally the one that I shall never forget.

What next? We were headed to Gangtok, Sikkim. Dad had been promoted to his new ranks and had been transferred to Gangtok. I don't know if he had been working closely towards his transfer to Gangtok, but apparently, on my way that day, I got the feeling that a bigger picture was being painted by my parents, which was yet to unfold. I waited patiently.

We were about nearing Rangpo, a small town midway to the capital city of Sikkim—Gangtok.

Dad asked me to pass him the bottle of water from the rear seat. Clearing his throat while I was busy fetching the bottle, he went on sharing his thoughts that both of them had plans of building a small house in one of the hill town—Kalimpong.

They told me they were in love with hills, and it was where their hearts belonged . . .

Dad asked me to share my thoughts on their decision.

'Do whatever that makes you happy' is what I really wanted to tell them . . . but, instead, something unexpected came out of my mouth. '*Hills sure do have a different energy which will make you understand why you need to spend more time with it.*'

My dad thought for a while and stated that it had been the best speech he had ever heard from me. He thought that I was shaping into a man he had envisioned me to be.

He never understood, I was only flowing with the moment and did not bother much on what they did . . .

Delhi, Delhi, Delhi, Delhi, Delhi—that was the only thing running in the channels of my head. You tune into a different frequency, switch the change button, and there it went again . . . Delhi . . . Delhi, Delhi . . . Delhi . . . It was broadcasting my only dream, far away from someone else's dream.

You see, you need to understand I was so desperate to be somewhere far away from Sir Major's imagination, and Delhi . . . I guess I was just saying things that made no sense to me, but I had painted a bigger picture in Sir Major's world.

We were almost at the last leg of our final uphill climb towards our destination, and Sir Major started talking again. I quickly assessed the temperature around and slipped my idea of moving to Delhi to pursue my further studies. What more, I used my mom's connection to prove that there were always someone to take care of me. Not sure what happened next, but Sir Major shared his thoughts—their (Mom and Dad's) initial intentions was to get me somewhere close by them, but they were convinced that boarding had done me mature enough, and they themselves were working on getting me enrolled in one of the reputed institutes of, down south, Bangalore.

Not what I exactly had on my mind, but I don't know why Mom was strongly against Delhi, and the only window available for me with my escape from an alternate reality was—Bangalore. Somehow my parents always thought that just like their decision to send me to a boarding had reaped its fruits, so shall sending me to Bangalore will do some good in shaping me to the person they finally wanted me to be.

The cards were flashed, and my parents were leading the game. I was packed within a week's time and was already heading towards the southern part of India. Not knowing that a new life was awaiting me, I silently landed on the land almost seven seas away—okay, that is too much of an exaggeration. Anyway it must be seven states away from the world I had left behind.

Got to count it someday?

I got myself in a fine institution that was reputed for its holistic development of an individual. *Whatever it meant by it?*

Anyway, talking about college, it was here where my learnings were tested to a new height. Suddenly, I found myself in a place where whatever I had learnt from my school days somehow made no further sense. Lessons were being questioned every time, and I failed to understand what was happening around me . . .

Then I slowly talked myself and reminded that, in time, the canvas would paint itself a fresh new portrait.

I started off with academics, and as always, it gave me no hope of finding the truth on reality. Then I took up games, and in time, moved on to rock and roll.

It was on stage where I found myself to be in a brand-new world. It brought me to a frame from where the faces around seemed to be a happier lot. Music spoke through every single face and even the souls who were running apart—they were brought together by a singing heart.

Life had just turned into a party that could not be missed any more.

Yes—all the while, we were taught how life was a big struggle, but here I had nothing to think about it any more, I managed my own okay.

So what if the money was coming from Sir Major's pocket, I still had to manage myself, and I was managing myself good and was able to meet with my needs every month.

Time had taught me the art of survival . . .

Sometimes life played lucky enough to earn a treat or to save up to ones meant for you and share every bit of your happiness with the energies around and sometimes dropping out from events where I had to turn to this fine gentleman who foots the bills—life had become a circus.

Music, on the other hand, gave me the existence that I had always craved for, and life was changing its colours. It brought me to a frame where everyone around me suddenly wore a friendly face. It helped bring in the souls that were previously unknown . . . closer to me.

Initially, they were bunch of eager journalists (gossiper) waiting to know more on my life. And as usual, my parents stole the limelight. Most of their inquiry on me stopped with their inquisitiveness to know more on my parents' love story.

Questions kept on flowing; how did they meet, was there any trouble for them initially, which language did I speak at home, what . . . ?

You know those usual questions I had been hearing throughout my life.

I realised that people around saw a different story in me. Maybe the realisation of this sudden shrinking of my world, even though it had expanded quite visibly must have made me stick around even more closely with the folks that shared some bit of a similar story with me.

Now when I look back through the pages of my life, I kind of felt that friends who shared some bit of similarity to my story might have felt the change in energy around them, and this could have been the reason why they opted to stay closer with familiar faces around.

The circle kept on growing. Though, in that portrait, I was still standing out a bit odd, but I was safely shaded by the illusion of belonging to a story familiar to me.

Any story that connected us with our forgotten days quickly became the base of our long-term camaraderie. During this process, we never realised that there were so many stories with each one of us to share together. It was all about getting to know each other.

Sometimes in-between stories, one could find their own connections. Somehow you could find yourself fit in that picture too. At times, it was the connections between various aspects from our previous life; and at times, stories from our school days made it tick. Sometimes the culture that we shared became the base of our friendship. It was a brand-new canvas that provided the space for others to come with their own story and build a new painting together. The circle only kept on growing, just like them creepers . . . it slowly but steadily had started to grow in our life.

Not even half as much time spent as compared to the school life, and my new existence had already built an army to feed with its memories.

Every afternoon, it appeared as if someone had called upon a meeting of the United Nations at the joint. Name it and you could almost find at least someone representing the county or the state in that small circle we shared—sitting and sharing a bit of their own story.

Okay, that is a bit too stretched again, but I guess you could find almost most of them belonging to some different part of this world.

'Explorers' written all over the face, the locals too participated at times to share the piece on their life's happenings.

I, of course, was a 'lightning Ninja'. The meetings, generally with quick humour as its favourite pastime, became a place to make connections and meet new faces. Somehow, I could slip away from the meetings in-between and catch up with fellows from the other parts that somehow got left out from the meetings at the United Nations.

They were the ones who remained far away from the circus and very much preferred to be left alone in their own little universe. Nothing could break them apart. So this is how I got to know a bit about everyone around, not just the ones loud and clear but the ones who remained silent too.

Most of the folks knew where exactly to find themselves during the college intervals—at the joint, of course, mostly with coffee and with bunch of jokes and stories of mischief in the air—the sketches of memories were slowly being drawn, and United Nation was only growing stronger.

But in those faces, some faces ensured to be a part of a better portrait in the album of my life.

Tseten Dorji—from Sikkim, also fondly referred to as Bhaichung by the locals. (The famous Indian footballer who also happened to be from the same place that Tseten came from.)

Now that I stressed my brains so much, I get the insight that Tseten was never into football. He had never played the game and yet he was what the crowd said so.

Viraj Tuladhar—gentleman from Nepal with dreams of his life cast in a milestone plan, written in a permanent ink. He was someone who knew what he exactly wanted from his life.

Samaira Rana and Sunaina Rana (Sunaina was better known as Naina)—Though they were identical twins, both the sisters had nothing in common apart from their physical appearance.

Oh! How could I forget Dechen Lhamu and her group of friends?

Although her visits were not so regular, she did make it a point to come along and spend her time at the United Nations congregations.

She came from the kingdom of dragons—Bhutan, and had studied in the hills during her childhood days. We had some of our friends in common, and this connection was enough for her to feel a part of my world.

Funny, now to think about it, but she is an important connection to the entire story ahead.

She used to have a regular entourage whenever she came by to visit us. I reckon this might have been her way of telling us that she was a force to be reckoned with. Her circle had Ben and Reni who hailed from the north-eastern part of India. They were folks with pretty simple thoughts and were good folks to have around.

Dechen also used to get her friend, a tall, dark-haired girl, Um! Can't seem to recollect her name? Okay! Let's keep her as tall, dark-haired girl for a while.

Tall, dark-haired girl—can't remember her name—was from Mumbai. A fair girl with dark long tresses to flaunt, she was a silent soul who ever did anything but speak. They were the regulars with Dechen during her visits. However, time in-between she used to manage to attach some wandering souls along with her.

Some of them turned out an absolute disappointment. Apologies for using such a dramatic word, but let the truth be told. I have been a little too considerate regarding this.

A larger imagination is required to further paint the pictures with the given words to aptly describe those few lost souls. Because, whenever they arrived, there was a sudden dip in energy around.

I was desperately trying to figure out the change in this energy level. Something told me then, what I had learnt so far was taking me nowhere.

Why is it not the way it used to be earlier? Why is there this sudden false understanding of what I knew so far had to be scrapped forever?

In time, I was to get the answer in style. The only thing I had to do then . . . was to wait . . .

It was Viraj's birthday, and a big party had been planned that night. The next day was a national holiday, and everyone's mood was running free and fun.

Party as much as we could and then sober it all the way to recovery the following day seemed to be the motto of the night then.

My humble soul reached five minutes ahead of the designated time. Viraj was running the last-minute errands before he closed his day and got ready for the show to begin.

Kabir! Someone shouted my name.

I turned around to see Dechen seated at the corner of the room, the cupboard in-between had been hiding her from my view. I had to stretch a little towards the left to catch a glimpse of her. There she was smiling at me.

It took a while after I settled next to her to realise that she was not alone. There was a gentleman right next to her.

She made the introduction; his name was Jacob Engel and apparently she was dating him. I was surprised that Dechen was dating a Westerner. Though she was liberal at heart, she was a bit orthodox when it came to her customs.

Trust me, she once mentioned about how she believed in her culture and would only follow what her parents have taught her—to be married into her fellow community.

Anyway who am I to judge?

And it was my turn to get introduced to Jacob, she went on . . .

'He is Kabir—Kabir Gurung, you can say he is my best friend.'

Um! I was buzzed for a moment. Best friend? Huh!?

Well, this was not the only surprise of the day.

Whatever Dechen meant by it, it looked like it eased the situation with Jacob, and maybe he saw me as 'less of a threat'. He instantly got glued to my friendship . . .

Before I could regain myself from what had just happened, I could see Jacob talking at length on his India discovery, and while he was counting back his memories and sharing his life's exceptional journey to the garden city of India, he was equally sad that his stay was nearing completion, and as his destiny had in store (in his own word) a mockery—he had to meet Dechen, the soulmate he had always been waiting forever.

About half an hour after hearing stories, it became clear how he had accidentally bumped into Dechen while he was at the college, trying to secure a seat for his sister, how in that blip of the eternity of time, they both had discovered they had so much in common, and just a few days back, they had finally made up their minds to know each other better. Here they were, yet another couple in love.

Apparently I got to know from him that his discovery of India had inspired his kid sister to travel all the way to India and pursue her higher studies from the country that was once known as the golden bird.

As this conversation was taking place, all I was wishing at that moment was for the party to kick-start. My heart was already in it and was desperately waiting for it to begin.

I was waiting for the music to hit the air, the madness to reach its limit, and happiness to be shared by all.

Just then Tseten entered along with Naina and Sumaira. Both dressed in a pretty summer wear, they were wearing white as their themed colour. They surely looked overtly dressed to prove that they were twins indeed. Silly of them, as if we could not figure out from their faces. Anyway, both knew what I thought about them, and there was nothing to hide. We were friends!

I was relieved to see them all. Dechen greeted everyone and took her turn to introduce her boyfriend Jacob with the rest of the folks. There were whispers slipping its way as she made the announcement. Jacob stood there as a mule and appeared as if he was being auctioned in an open market. Silent unspoken stories were flashing from scanning eyes around him, and this might have caught hold of the good atmosphere around Jacob's universe—he was breathing heavily.

I could sense trouble with him, and just when his legs were about to give him up and let him down, I caught hold of him.

'Goddarnit! What is wrong?' Dechen screamed.

'Jacob . . . Jacob . . .'

There was the voice that pierced my ears like an icy knife. I turned around to see a fairly tall, white-skinned, red lipped, blue-eyed, and blonde-haired . . .

What? Okay, who is this? And why does she have to scream so loud? No one's dead!

I shoved her little to make some room to lay down Jacob and give him space to catch up with the air. *In a moment of anxiety I had unknowingly pushed the fair lady.*

'Stop pushing me!' There was a loud shout . . .

'I am sorry, I didn't mean to . . .'

'Whatever?' . . . came the next response.

I was amazed at the way she behaved.

'Maybe, she must have thought I had pushed her on purpose? Maybe that might have ticked her nerve. Oh! Anyway I did not know who she was . . . She must be one of the members belonging to Dechen's outfit. Let it go, and everything will be fine,' I told myself to quiet my mind.

Jacob regained his composure and, looking a little embarrassed, chuckled!

Naadiaa!—sounded more like, 'Naah diaa' the way it was called.

It must have been the hard German accent that made them pronounce such a beautiful name the way they did. As for me, it stayed as Nadja—(Nadya), forever on my mind the moment she spelt it out.

She walked towards Jacob and smiled, while making faces as if she had just witnessed the biggest disgrace of the century.

Jacob quickly grabbed his coat and hugged her. She was smiling all the while.

Dechen stood there smiling, I could not understand.

After almost five long minutes of hush talks with her, Jacob turned around and introduced me to her.

'Kabir, meet my sister, Nadja . . .'

Before even I could say anything, she said, 'Hi, I am Nadeeya.' She went off.

'Nadya?' I returned.

'No, pronounce it as "Naid-ya".'

'How do you spell it?'

'N-A-D-J-A.'

'That's Nad-Ya, simple as it is spelt. Maybe it might have to do something with their accent that gave funny sounds whenever they called names,' I joked to myself quietly.

As the story goes, Nadja had been acting weird all that night. She would be fine moments before I showed up, and as soon as she had me within her view, some kind of weird evil took refuge in her. Every time around her a sudden change of energy flowed to which I was being slowly made aware. For a while, I thought, she was still mad with me for pushing her.

'Time to buckle up and take the party to some other place,' I told myself.

I took my exemption from Viraj for an early exit and made my way to meet my school friend Nirpesh at his place. He was in a different college and had been calling me for some time to come visit his humble aboard.

'So be it, they were the brothers who had walked shoulder to shoulder during my childhood days. Good time to meet them,' I reminded myself and moved on.

I reached Nirpesh's house around eleven at night, and it looked as if there was a party going on at his place as well. He had never mentioned about the party but was very specific on asking me to be present at his place on that very day. I had completely forgotten about it and had instead been busy planning Viraj's birthday celebration.

All within a night, I found myself amusing myself in another get-together.

When I entered, it seemed the party had already reached half way through, and the spirits to uplift one's soul were already running short.

There were faces unseen before at Nirpesh's place.

I was walking towards the kitchen when Nirpesh appeared from the restroom. He was in high spirit and went shouting out loud the moment he saw me.

I went ahead and handed him the wine, which I had swiftly picked up on the way to his place. He mentioned that it was his birthday and had organised a small get-together for his close friends and wanted me to be a part of it too.

Close shave, good that I made it. I congratulated him and wished him happiness ahead.

Nirpesh took me to the main hall and got me introduced to his friends.

It was that night at his place that I met Simran.

Simran had this bright shining face, with no signs of cosmetic to enhance her beauty; her only accessory was the broad-framed black spectacles she wore. She was a smart, intelligent, and beautiful soul. I also learnt that she was not only academically brilliant, but she was also heavily into history and music.

As we spoke that night, there were topics to be covered, and time was running short.

We wished there were ways to stop the time or somehow convert seconds into minutes and minutes into hours.

The night had grown heavier, and people rationed to battle the party of the freedom midnight, had started to retire to their dreamland. They had started to fall asleep—one by one.

Simran and I stood still, cracking up at smallest things we had to share before the night also grew heavier on her, and she made her exit.

On my way home that night, thoughts started to clog my mind . . . 'Who is she? Simran, I didn't even care to ask her for her contact details. Anyway, what could I do now? All I knew about her was her first name and one night of chat.'

(It would be a long interval in time before I met Simran again.)

I reached home and found my flatmates in deep sleep. Silently I made my way through the hallway. It was pitch-dark, and there was no electricity at home. Trying not to disturb anyone, I slowly crept behind the couch and made my way towards my room.

There was a loud shout yelling and cursing my relatives and anyone that could have come close to my relation. I realised I had stamped on Adit's hand. No one else but him had the skills to make such a cruel remark in its most creative and poetic form.

Adit—Aditya Khanna—Mom's elder brother's son . . .

Initially Mom's family had opposed her marriage with Dad and had disowned her as my dad belonged to a different community . . . but later, in time, her parents realised their mistake and Mom was allowed to re-establish connections with her roots again.

'What Adit is doing here at the hall and not sleeping on his own bed?'

Well, he always had his explanations to his weird behaviour so I chose not to get into it.

Adit, reducing the volume and grieving in pain, asked me as to what I was up to at such an early hour of the day. I informed him that I was returning from a friendly gathering and was headed towards my room and was hoping not to disturb anyone.

I told him that lighting up the hallway was also not an option as the electricity had been disconnected at our place. We had failed to pay the bill on time, which of course was the result of Adit's negligence to his duty. It was his turn to clear the bills, and as reality had doubted before, we were left to darkness—thanks to him.

He promised he would get the arrears cleared at the earliest in his half-awakened state; I believed him.

The next three days, there was still no electricity at home.

For a while, we had the most romantic dinner at our place. Yes, the ones with the candles lit around. Didn't matter what was there on the plate, the ambience was romantically dimmed to hide away the reality from us.

Our hearts were somewhere else while we finished our meal, just like good old romance.

Had it not been for the other flatmate who was always up for an action, I guess the drama between Adit and me would have landed us in darkness for a longer period.

Surprisingly this time, it took him several days to get it fixed, what he generally did within hours of darkness. I was surprised as it was a big change to see Bhasker wait for so long.

Bhasker Barua from Assam was the other flatmate living with us during our college days.

We shared a two-bedroom, hall, and a kitchen with a common bathroom. There was a small study area, just enough to dump a single soul into it.

Question was, who was ready to fit in?

While Adit and I were fighting for rooms, Bhasker had quietly made the study his hiding place. He never complained about the space he got. That would always be me, moving things around to create an illusion of something new in life. Every time!

The college reopened after a short interval; the air was charged with energy from the lectures slipping through the classrooms.

I could sense a sudden change in the energy around.

'What happened to me?'

I gave myself the permission to exempt myself from the rest of the class for that day and was seated in the cafeteria—sipping a cup of tea—heavily lost in my own thoughts.

Tseten sneaked up from behind and startled me. The coffee was all over my pants. Seconds later, Nadja walked in and, looking at me, passed a snide remark.

'Looks like someone could not make it in time.'

I looked at her, and she was with Dechen and was staring at me at that moment. Dechen laughed and offered me some paper whites to clean the mess.

(Nadja had joined the same college that we were in and had become a part of Dechen's entourage.)

Suddenly fear, at a pace of a light, pierced through my heart. The air grew cold; my heart was out of its natural rhythm.

What was happening? I had never felt so nervous before in my life. I looked at Dechen—I felt fine and then I looked at Tseten—I was still all good.

Then again, I heard Nadja passing another remark of hers . . . Her lips were moving involuntarily, but none of the words could be heard. My hands were covered in sweat, and my lips fluttered uncontrollably, but my face—it wore a smile that could be taken by none.

'What's happening?'

I thought I had learnt everything during my schooling days, and what was so different that I could not be myself again? Why was I being bullied the way I was, why was I taking it the way I did, and why was I being pushed around? Unwanted attention, and I was dealing with it. These were the questions that did not seem to find any anchor then.

I ignored Nadja and went on with my usual self. Naina also joined the circus a while later, and soon, a whole other folks would join the circus.

It seemed there was some prayer meeting for the teachers, and the classes had been called off for the day. After spending an hour, Tseten and I decided that a game of snooker would be the only indulgence at that time that could rescue our lazy little soul.

With all the care left behind, we took off to test our skills in the game of snooker. Wagers running high and pride to be fed with victory, the game began. It was almost 5 p.m. when the scores looked somewhat—four is to two against Tseten; Tseten requested to call it a day.

While exiting the joint, I met Rajdeep, a newly grown acquaintance from the party at Nirpesh's.

Oh! How could I forget, the one with whom Simran had come to that party?

He asked me where I had disappeared towards the later part of that night.

There I told you before, about 'lightning Ninja'. Well, I never told him that I was with Simran, chatting up with her. Wicked!

As we went ahead with our conversation, I got to know more about Simran from him.

She was a first year student at the women's college close by. A religious Punjabi girl from Chandigarh, she was someone who always knew what she wanted from life, and somewhere behind her mind, she always knew that her intuitions never failed her.

Surprisingly, when I recollect our conversation at the party that night, I realised that we had spoken very less about each other and had discussed more of history and music only.

That was the only connection that we had in common; we had never discussed on our personal likes and dislikes, and here I was getting those information from someone— possibly it could have been her boyfriend himself.

Later when Rajdeep's conversation caught a little extra mile, I understood that Rajdeep's and Simran had been childhood friends and had been brought up like brother and sister.

Rajdeep's dad had got transferred to Bangalore and had later made the garden city as their permanent residence.

Simran had joined them after completing her high school and was studying business.

Thanks to a sudden meeting of Rajdeep, I got to know more about Simran—where she studied and her likes and dislikes. I also got to know her complete name: Simranjeet Chopra.

As the named played in my mind, I stood there still for a while, and in that very few seconds of my life, I once again felt a sudden change in energy around me, and once again I was found unable to understand the given circumstance.

'What was so different now that left me so vulnerable? I was plagued with paralysis of thoughts and failed to understand why the theories built after so many effective experiments during our school days were working no more. The answer was to come in next few hours.'

After parting our ways with Rajdeep, Tseten and I went to Café Coffee Day to grab chilled ice coffee before retiring home. As we made our way inside the coffee shop, Tseten realised that Naina and Sumaira were also at the same coffee shop and quickly went by them to greet.

Dechen was also there, and next to her was Nadja. I went up to say my hellos and proceeded to get my order placed.

Naina shouted from a distance and asked me to join them once the order was done.

Tseten saw this and walked to me. He was a bit different while he spoke, jealousy spat right out of his words. Even before I could say something, words that were sharper than knives were being aimed at me, thrown at rates which could even shy away the Kalashnikovs. It took a while for Tseten to calm down.

Sumaira looked a bit concerned. Naina, as always, did not see anything in the picture. Dechen was concerned as hell, I realised. No one heard what Tseten had to say, but everyone around sensed the sudden freezing moments in the air.

I quickly pulled aside Tseten and asked him what the matter was.

Tseten moved to hide behind the pillar and, in a very dejected tone, stated that he loved Naina a lot. He was angry, angry because no matter what, he failed to get Naina's attention the way he wanted it to be.

My mind cleared; it was like one of the green traffic signals in the Bangalore City. The ones that only comes up once in a while and stays green for longer than you would have expected.

It was then when I realised it was jealousy that had turned out to be a friend's enemy.

'What was suddenly different for me now?'

Well, of course, the other part of reality I had ignored before; there were girls around who had become friends and were sharing the common frame that drew up our paintings then, and they came in a different form of energy.

Suddenly, the issue was about the co-existence.

Science has taught that whenever there are two or more different types of energies present, all it takes is for nature to play the catalyst.

It explained a lot about the sudden dip in the energy around. Yup, they were different species with different rules book hanging by them. This one was unknown to a mankind, subject given up by learned scholars. Who are we to question?

Not that we had not met their form before, it was just that I had never really paid attention to them.

As I rested my thoughts, while the ladies were busy trying to figure out what happened minutes back. I was sitting there, smiling on the revelation of life and was thinking about the details I had gathered on Simran.

Fate had it, it was only after two years Simran and I would cross our path again. This was not clear at that point of time. I only knew she was someone that I had met, whom I shall be remembering for a long time.

I quickly got sucked into the constant demands of the college life. I got busy trying to get decent academic scores to keep unwanted surveillance from Sir Major at bay, at the same time juggling to be the boy that I had always been, it was difficult times for me then.

My heart spoke music and poetry; and my duty as a son was forcing me to shine our family values even higher.

The man I was being shaped was happy having born, every moment, while mould of the man I was supposed to be was hanging around the wall at my home.

A kirpan, a gift to me from my uncle and a khukuri next to it; both the pieces are a reminder of the person I am always to be.

3

I really don't have a count on how the year after the first in Bangalore fared. I remember it start and then suddenly we were hanging towards the closing month.

What I do recollect of it is by the year end, the United Nation started to grow even much fatter. Guess the fresh new arrivals had found a place to feel together. My visits had seen a sharp decline at the United Nation's congregations.

What was I doing?

Oh yes, rock and roll. We were busy covering gigs all over the colleges, participating and having a gala time with our music. Guitar became my regular affair and was my friend who spoke on behalf of me; it never complained.

Guitar—was the friend who spoke my mind. She was my best friend.

Anyway, I did end up meeting quite a lot of new faces that year. In that crowd, I met a few who had their own charm or a story they brought along.

It was one of the shows in which we had to perform, and the venue was a women's college, at least eight kilometres away from ours. Those days the only cheapest mode of transport for a student was a bus.

But there we were, ready to take an auto all the way for an eight-kilometre ride. (Priceless)

The auto driver demanded Rs. 50—a round figure for their convenience.

I argued that it would take half of what he had just mentioned to reach us to our destination.

The air was already heated with the unpredictable Bangalore sun.

'Comes up whenever it feels like and disappears to let the sky cry for a while, then suddenly the rays from it warm up everything around as if nothing had happened minutes before.'

I told my mates to ignore the auto driver and see if there could be some other arrangements.

Sanjeev was quick with his response, 'How about a bullock cart?'

Sanjeev was the vocalist of the band and was always quick with his wit.

I didn't find him funny at that moment.

We had to reach the venue before noon, and there we were arguing with auto drivers, just to reach us to our requested destination.

There were statements flying around. Statements, such as, we were merely students and were not earning to shell out as much as we wished we could.

Someone even went Bollywood on them, 'Just because the college is well known does not mean my dad owns some kind of factory and sends notes packed in suitcases to us.'

Our arguments were falling on deaf ears. Just to add to our misery, the other auto fellows wanted to take a dig on us too. As the heat was slowly rising, another auto approached us, as if he was an angel who had come to our rescue, quickly parked next to us, and inquired as to where we wanted to go.

'Vasanthnagar, bhaiya!'

This one demanded Rs. 100, ridiculous!

Sanjeev got on his humorous best and said to the autowala, 'Chennai jayega (Will you go to Chennai for that amount)?'

I could sense this was a useless chat leading us nowhere. I crossed the road and got the band members to the other side and stopped an auto. Thanks to our luck, we managed to secure it, and this one was ready to take us for as much as the meter ticked up for reaching us our destination.

I knew a shortcut that would cut right through the main road that took us towards the direction that we were headed to.

With a quick instruction to the auto driver, soon we were on our way to the venue where we were to perform.

On our way, we all remained silent till we reached the gates of the venue.

All sussed out, I told myself it was time to let my guitar talk.

The entire hall was packed to its capacity, and the noise was constant and deafening. I could barely hear myself in that crowd.

We plugged our instruments and gave a final check.

Sanjeev, with his high-pitched voice shouted, 'Are you with me?' The crowd responded with a loud yes.

'Are you really with me?'

Another loud cheer from the crowd, and it set my blood pumping. There were lights hitting my eyes so hard, I could see nothing in front of me. At that moment, it only appeared to me I was covered in a bright shining light, and everything around me was dark and empty.

The guitar screeched, and the drums rolled, we were singing songs—rock and roll. And when we left, the crowd was left asking for more.

After leaving the rock and roll avatar on stage, I packed my guitar inside its case and asked my fellow mates to take care of my belongings.

I had to pay a visit to the rest room.

You see, the pressure of being on a stage is always demanding, and one needs to hold on for a very long time and then rush to get the release.

Nervous, oh no, who's nervous? I was just highly hydrated before kicking around on the stage.

While I was done with my business and was washing myself clean, I heard a sweet voice with guitar strumming in its background; it sounded like an angel's harp. It slowly built up its pace, where the mellow voice suddenly turned expressive and was running violent, filled with pain and loneliness. Maybe it was also the way each word was narrated while she sang; the entire story was silently expressed as the voice went humming to its end.

Music had touched me that day, and I had fallen in love with it.

I walked my way to the auditorium, and the voice grew even sweeter and loud. The words so crisp, it crackled the air, and the guitar gave a constant company with the flow of its sweet notes to the voice that had shamed the angels. I shall never forget.

I took the back door to get next to the stage, and as I walked in, I looked towards the stage. Our eyes met for a brief moment before we both looked away.

(Rachel! She's Rachel Miller, she is representing her college the one that is hosting the event. I must say she is gifted with her voice. Her dad is from Great Britain and Mom, a Goan. They have a reputed restaurant in central Bangalore.) Sanjeev carried on . . .

He had been giving me all the required information even without asking him for any. But I was happy inside as I wanted to get to know more about Rachel.

Rachel was born and raised in Bangalore and had known Sanjeev as they had gone to the same school during their childhood days in Bangalore.

'She was of an average built, reflecting dark hair, her voice could shame the angels in the heaven, and her smile could bring the innocence of a child to anyone she looked at.'

'Look at her, boy, isn't she beautiful? Look at her, Kabir.'

'Huh, Sanjeev, that's an awful lot of information on Rachel that you have got.' I winked!

Sanjeev looked at me and said, 'That is Rachel we are talking about, Kabir. You just need to know her and then only shall you know what I am telling you about.'

'Do you love her?' I went on to ask him . . .

He responded that he did love her and paused for a while . . . The pause felt like an eternity to me, and my heart was already pounding and would have burst open any moment.

And then he continued, 'I do love her for the person she is. She is like my little sister.'

Relieved! For a moment, I had lost my creative self to deal with the shock of thinking Sanjeev was into Rachel.

'What did Sanjeev say? Oh yes, I have to know her.'

I found her backstage, packing up her instruments.

I congratulated her for an awesome show and introduced myself to her.

She said she knew who I was and had been following our music for some time.

'Moment to pull your chest out.'

It wasn't really one of those moments. I don't know, but I was talking very less at that time.

Rachel went on sharing her thoughts on my guitar solos. She went on to tell me that it was as if the guitar was speaking what my heart wanted to say . . .

'Where was this coming from? Okay, she is being nice?'

I thanked her for her sweet remark and went to share my thoughts about her singing. I told her that she had a voice that I shall never forget . . . Whatever that meant? May be I got nervous.

I swear I saw her blushing when I told her that, and she chose to acknowledge it with her silence.

Just then, the results of the fest were announced. Rachel had won the competition for best music, and we stood second. I strongly felt the decision was wise; she had won without any competition.

Don't think I am supporting her because of the way I felt for her, trust me, you had to be there to hear her sing. Magic!

Once she was back receiving her trophy; I had this boiling compulsion to reach out to her, one last time before I left the drama behind.

'So did I listen to myself then?'

Before I could even decide, I was standing right next to her. I stood there, frozen.

'Say something, idiot', I told myself, but my lips refused to move and my eyes, they were not even blinking anymore? I had been staring straight at her.

'Kabir, are you all right?' Rachel caught my hand.

There you go. I can never really explain what happened next; never had I experienced such a force before. No! It was not covered in any of the syllabus so far nor had I been educated on this one before.

But if you really want to know what happened next, all I am saying is . . .

'Music touched my lips that night.'

What next? We found ourselves sharing a canvas of life and were found mostly painting it with colours from our good memories.

She was a kind-hearted and beautiful soul.

She was brilliant with her thoughts and could shame anyone moments before they even realised.

She loved my songs and often told me that she was crazy about the flow of notes in my composition—she said that it cuts so interestingly the meaning between melodies, and it always pierced her mind like an atomic explosion.

She was also a critic of my songs and would give her feedback with all the cruelty left in her. She was honest all the time, which I cannot deny.

I still can't figure out how and why we drifted away in life. Sadly, our journey only lasted for about a year.

Maybe, in time, I was to know. Maybe that is why they say 'Everything happens for a reason.'

While stories with Rachel were being painted, there were stories of me being written in a different world. I had my existence there too. How can I forget about it completely? I had to get my graduation degree too to earn.

'Love has its own place,' I always told my mind. *I know my thoughts are a little heavy to digest at the moment . . . but the stories are not just one sided at times.*

Cafeteria and the old schools seated on the hang-out area reflected a regular picture. It was our second year in the college, and with friends around, life seemed to be rolling on fair.

Oh no, not again, there she was . . . Dechen with her entourage was visiting the United Nations.

No, don't get me wrong, it was not that I was not happy to see her but what she brought along,—Nadja—she was with her as well.

(I don't know what, but there was something in me that she could not stand; whenever I was around, it changed her to a person that everyone was rather surprised to see. I was always caught with the guilt that she had not forgiven

me for how our initial meeting went by. Dark, cold energy flowed into my universe as soon as she appeared before me.)

Quick hellos were exchanged and boy, had she had to speak again.

'I hear your girlfriend sings real well, bet you hit the lottery?'

Nadja, why does she have to comment every single time, why?

I fail to understand her character; just because I kept shut did not mean that I had no reply to fit her remarks.

Why does she do this? Why

I turned around to see it was rather Naina who had joined the ranks and had passed the smart comment.

I saw Nadja standing silent. She was looking at me, with questions in her mind, maybe trying to figure out what would be my response.

True, she was not the one who was pressing the air around me this time.

I was surprised it was Naina.

You see, she was a close friend of mine. She was like the boys who had walked shoulder to shoulder without questioning one's integrity. I could not figure what had dwelled on her that made her act the way she did then.

Anyway, I sat there silent . . . Tseten came to my rescue and dragged me away. Apparently his dad had sent him some extra cash for him to splurge around. He had planned to pick up some pants and a pair of shoes. Probably if any cash left after his initial wish list was fulfilled, he had plans to buy some Ts along.

While exploring the shops around, Tseten met his childhood friend. It seemed like they were meeting after a long time, and as for me, I was standing on the road, looking as dumb and as oblivious as I could be.

Tseten nudged me and introduced me to him.

I don't know what happened next, but Tseten turned into this generous person and offered to treat us with a round of drink to celebrate the moment.

'Celebrate the moment,' that is what he said.

What next, we were busy bingeing at a pub.

Foods were flying off the menu and drinks never seemed to run out. Three of us drank to our heart's content that night.

(I thought we had just gone for a round of drinks. But as long as someone was treating, our hearts never complained.)

As a direct result of our unplanned bingeing; I had to take refuge at Tseten's place that night—we reached his place with our senses left at the bar.

The next day, Tseten woke up with his head running on overdrive.

His heart was working extra hard that morning to push the bloods to his brain; instead, alcohol fumes gushing through his blood were reaching the brain, just a little ahead in time, and it gave him a terrible headache.

He dragged himself to the mirror and stood there staring at himself. He then reached for his purse and slowly opened it.

Initially, there was a grin on his face. He then looked towards his left, turned right, and put his wallet away.

He must have realised, he had wasted all the cash given to him by his dad; the pants, the shoes, and the extra Ts: they all vanished overnight, and the only remembrance of what was left of it had already been flushed away in the toilet early morning by him.

I think it must have been a deep seated-guilt that made Tseten come over the next day asking if I could spare him Rs. 200. I gave him the amount, and he disappeared for a while and returned with a nice white T later. He promised to repay my money as soon as possible.

(He was promising me to return my money back after spending almost a fortune on us, celebrating the evening before. It was Rs. 200 that he had borrowed from me. Do I trust him?

Of course, yes . . .)

But I hope you understand when you are surviving on a sum that has been legally agreed upon with your parent, studied carefully and drawn upon conclusion and for their victory, it had been topped up with a buffer, say plus 500, before the final figure is arrived and handed over to you, it means you have no room to make mistakes. If any, you are on your own.

(So I do hope you understand the value of Rs. 200 back then. Why would I not question anyone before handing them over my money? But then, Tseten was a friend whom you could count upon.)

Parents, do they have any idea about miscellaneous expenses while growing up?

(We need money for our drinks, parties, clubbing, dinner, and lunch at a decent restaurant, movies, snooker, and the list goes on.)

Okay, those were just my dreams. But we need money to survive, to pay the rents, bills, transportation, and food. You see there are lots to be taken care of.

Of course, I did not mention 'dating'. It would have started a World War III if my parents got to know about it. *Yup—one of the few expenses that go unaccounted, as the accountant himself is busy feasting on his imagination.*

I got back my money a week later from Tseten, it helped me push a beautifully planned evening with Rachel. It was a romantic date. We met at Church Street and headed for a Chinese lunch. Damages covered within Rs. 120. I can't believe we could buy a wholesome lunch with the kind of money those days. Now a single dish would dish you out more than the entire bills we used gather back then. I returned home 'happy and rich' with Rs. 80 still in my pocket.

I was proud of my management skills . . .

Another mundane day at college, and I was bored attending classes, and my heart was hanging in the cafeteria.

It was lunch time, and I was waiting for Viraj to join me for lunch, but he was held back with some class work. Tseten had planned to stay away from college that day; he was arranging Naina's birthday bash.

(Actually, I never understood his logic. He was setting up a surprise birthday party for Naina and had asked Sumaira to help him with the arrangements.)

Thought, both were twins, and it would have meant Sumaira's birthday too.

'God help my friend.'

But later I got the update on the recent developments that were happening silently in the frame that I had been sharing with my college friends.

Sumaira had found her soul mate in a junior of the same college; Naina had finally succumbed to Tseten's proposal. It had been a week since both had started going around.

It appeared to me that I had missed out a lot, but I was happy with the paintings that I had been drawing with Rachel around . . .

There was love all around me . . .

The year went by quick with plenty of interesting stories to share.

There were stories that taught me something new, stories that lasted a month or two, stories of arrival, and the stories of departure still being written, life as a circus never seemed to cease.

(Some souls were busy rejoicing, while some silently moved on, and for a few, they were just too involved with others' life to see things around themselves. *Then the day came by, a long summer break before the final season of our college stories began. Stories of home had become a part of every single topic for discussion—it had started a month ago. With this, the time had come for everyone to make their journey to their loved ones. They soon packed their bags home.)*

As for me, I stayed back in Bangalore as Rachel was nearing her departure. I gave an excuse of taking up a coaching class to Sir Major, and he bought it.

There I was spending every single minute of my time left with Rachel, while rest of the folks went to their home, visiting their parents.

Time had made me forget the reality. Rachel was a batch senior to me, and she had plans to migrate to London. It had been her childhood dream to pursue her higher studies from the country where her dad belonged and had been working ever since her early age to realise her dream.

Soon the day would arrive when she would make the journey far, far away from my life.

I don't know what it was with me, but I convinced myself that if Rachel followed her dreams, it would be the best for both of us.

I needed her right next to me, and there I was, asking her to follow her dreams.

Time spent with Rachel taught me a lot. It taught me about things probably I would have never realised.

Had I not met her, I would never have learnt what I had to learn then. She taught me about being human and human relationship, and above all, she taught me about love.

For the first time, I realised what it meant to lose someone.

Time came by soon when Rachel boarded her flight to London. She hugged me before proceeding towards the check-in area. She came back and hugged me even tighter. I laughed, and before she left for the final time, she kissed me and said she would miss me. I could not say the same to her. (She knew I would always miss her.)

We reminded each other to remain in touch; and so did we both for a while. We wrote to each other, spoke sometime in-between; but the distance seemed to have played its natural order.

I wrote to her, and it would be months before I would hear back from her. Sometimes, the phone network would play the devil and sometimes, the service charges.

(Another important thing to keep in mind, those days incoming calls were charged too. And if I am not mistaken, it must have cost rupees six a minute for every incoming call. The cell phone used to be right in front of me and the validity of the call services—all over. With limited money to get the recharge done, she would at times be unable to reach me.)

At first, I am sure we both realised the changes; slowly we got adjusted in time until we heard from each other no more and went with our lives ahead.

Rachel had silently been there in my life, without any melodrama or attention.

We had our own story; the picture in our memories sketched by us together remained engraved in time. Sadly, it had to end the way it did.

4

While everyone was returning from their home, gearing up for the final league of the college days, I was returning back from Goa.

After Rachel left, I had about three weeks before the college reopened, and since I was doing nothing, I went back, packing to Goa.

Where did I get the money from?

Sir Major was requested to deposit Rs. 6,000 towards the welfare fund of coaching classes, which I never got myself enrolled to.

Goa was out of the world. Upon reaching Goa, the energy around was completely different, and for a moment, I felt Goa belonged to a different universe. The places were packed with travellers and party revellers from all around the world. It was an amusement park where one could find characters dressed in Halloweens, bikers riding their way through the footpath and narrow roads, bartenders kept showing off their mixing skills, and bunch of folks were found running wild on the dance floor—high on nothing. I never wanted to return.

I took a bike to a cliff on a full-moon night, the seas were crashing down below, and the atmosphere was lit bright yellow.

I was busy searching for the party, the one the old reveller had mentioned to me at the beach.

(He mentioned that every full moon night, a feast was conceived to please the universe, and it happened in a secluded beach in-between Anjuna and Vagator. No one knew much about the party; it was a low-key, select few entry sort of an affair. That was what I had been told and what I was exactly looking forward to find myself at.)

Yes, the curious mind again.

I parked my bike at the cliff and started walking down the hill towards the beach. I climbed a small rock from where the sharp descent began. I could hear music in the air, sounds of gossips playing around, and a faint dim light simmering from the left corner of the beach. I had finally arrived at the venue, the one the Old Russian was talking about.

When I reached the venue, I realised the party was for anyone who could make it through the adventure in time. Every soul who could make it there was welcomed unconditionally. There were no special check points at the entry of the venue, and I walked in smooth. No one stopped me or asked me for an ID.

The people attending the party were in their merry best; none gave a look, with their face that spoke—I care.

All enjoying the beats that was floating in the air, it was as if the night had been drenched in a heavenly message coming from the music that was being played from the DJ's table.

DJ—he smiled wicked . . .

Trippy it was.

The sky turned purple, the forest dark green, the people dressed as Venetians, water shining silver while reflecting moonlit dream . . . festival was Goa's everyday affair.

———⋘———

The memory of fun in Goa was short-lived, and I found myself in the bus headed to Bangalore. The college would reopen in a few days.

My mood then could not be expressed in words. Bangalore would only remind me of Rachel, and Goa had brought me to a brand-new world.

Oh! How I felt then cannot be expressed.

My thought had taken me faster than I had thought would generally take to reach Bangalore. I was thinking all about my adventure in Goa, and the bus had already arrived in Bangalore. The conductor gave me a real good jolt and reminded me that it was the last stop for the bus, and it would not move further.

Bangalore! I caught an auto and went straight home. Adit had returned from his parents' home, and Bhasker was on his way back from his home.

Adit and I sat down sharing our recent experiences. Later in the evening, Adit talked me into attending a party at his friend's place. I agreed to join him.

From what I had seen last, the real parties happened in Goa. Somehow the parties in Bangalore had lost its charm. Especially after the night-curfew imposed in the Bangalore City, I felt the party life had begun to embarrass the true Bangaloreans.

Since the establishments are shut before the Cinderella time, everyone preferred to remain home and gather around in circles and call it a party. They chatted, drank, snacked, ate, chatted, and danced—all in the luxury of their so-called home.

(Bangalore parties had started to see a dramatic change in time. From being a free world, it had now turned into a regulated sad affair. But in Goa, one just got unified with the energy around and could feel the moment being created.)

One more loss added to the story of Bangalore. The party has started to suck. Big time!

I dragged my way through that night and was happy to be home at last. Called it a good night with Adit and went to bed.

College reopened, and it was the first day of our final year in college. Eager to meet the fellows who had been missing out in action for some time, visiting their loved ones, I quickly found myself back in college and instinctively walked to the cafeteria.

They were there, every one of them, shining even brighter. It must have been the effect from the meals they had taken—fresh from their mother's kitchen, some complained about their sudden weight gain, and some were a happy lot to have had a good feast back home.

Stories were making rounds, and everybody was in a rush to publish theirs first. As for me, I felt like I had just walked into a mental asylum that was freshly being built right in front of our own eyes.

A lot to catch up with from where we last left . . .

Tseten and Naina were still going strong. Tseten later admitted that he did not understand why Naina had suddenly started to annoy him a lot.

He did not want to lose her, but something about Naina had started to bother him constantly, and he felt Naina was not treating him right.

After listening to him for a while, the thoughts that were restrained by my tongue earlier went off like a bullet that was meant to be shot one fine day.

Have you imagined how many bullets are just lying in some cupboard for many years and how it must be getting rusted?

No, this would not be the one; it went off right through piercing Tseten's heart . . .

I told him that if Naina's beauty was what made him fall in love with her, I reminded him that he had a second chance. 'Her sister, Sumaira, is just a copy of her. Why won't you consider it? Guess she already likes you.'

Sarcasm must have been born when angel chose to smile at the devil's performance.

(I was only reminding Tseten to wake up . . . He was not in love with her but was merely infatuated to her beauty.)

Tseten frowned and sat quietly; moments later, he admitted it was for the way Naina spoke to everyone, and not just a few, that made him like her. He found her very kind and generous and had always wanted to know her better.

I had read him wrong, he was indeed in love with Naina, and I the smart brain had hurt him with my suggestion of him dating Sumaira.

But at that point in time, the reality screamed a different story in front of everyone to which Tseten chose to remain oblivious; Tseten was just a convenience for Naina.

(Even though it was clear that Naina was not really interested in Tseten, I remained silent for the love Tseten had for her. What was on Naina's mind? I really didn't know . . .)

I could not tell anything to comfort Tseten's heart; we both allowed the topic to fade away and pretended to listen to what others had to share.

By the way, how can I leave out Dechen and her stories? She spoke about her visit to her home—the land of the thunder dragon.

How she and her cousins took off on a holiday trip from Bhutan to Kathmandu—Nepal; she spoke about the friends she had not visited for decades and their meeting turning into an emotional saga . . . She went on adding with her adventure stories . . .

She also spoke about Jacob returning back to his own country and their fate hanging on the mercy of time.

There was a moment of pause from Dechen while she was still gathering her breath to start off narrating more of her sad stories; Nadja was quick with her 'hello' to me. She was smiling when she greeted me.

I turned around to carefully read through her, but the smile on her face got me blank. *Why there was a smile on her face, God only knew.*

I smiled back at her and asked how about her vacation.

I really don't know what I was saying then.

(Must have been that smile that got me off balance, I wasn't using my head.)

Nadja told me that she was on an adventure, exploring all over India. She did not want to go home; she thought it would be better to see more of India and its diverse cultures while she was already here.

She said there was something about India that made her feel she was here to find something profound, something that would remain forever in her life; she was searching to be enlightened.

Enlightened by what? I am sure she must have been equally unaware.

Interesting! Never knew she thought the way she did. All I could hear from her so far had been only the loathing words pouring from her mouth. This was new . . .

Dechen was silently observing the whole drama and lagging behind with her own thoughts, somehow managed to reach our conversation. She too found it funny. She had a grin on her face; it badly wanted to burst into a loud laughter; but she held it on her throat as long as she could; before finally breaking it into a coughing like sound to hide her actual intentions.

(Just like me, she had also grown into the understanding of Nadja not being good to me, and this sudden change in energy flow in-between us had her wits also cleaned white.)

Dechen had always mentioned that Nadja was an excellent girl, and she was never the way with anyone as she was with me. However, when it came to me, I had something in me that always caught her nerves.

(I guess most of the folks around, by now, also started to sense the change in the flow of currents between me and Nadja. There used to be a sudden surge in voltage every time we both got together; damages always reported beyond repair. That day she was right in front of me, and I didn't feel anything. Suddenly she had turned into this new person—someone I knew.)

Everyone looked at me with their ever-questioning eyes. Questions running in their head—how come?

I had no words or expression to answer them. Just by the look in my eyes, I told them, neither did I know anything about it. I too was confused.

'What had happened to Nadja during her India exploration that got her so nice to me?' Thoughts were running havoc in my head for some time.

Anyway, I reminded myself—and thanked God.

Good for me—one less soul from hating. I welcomed the change.

Nadja then asked me as to what I had been up to during the vacation. I told her about my Goa story, skipped Rachel's part, I don't know why. Did not feel like picking up her topic then; it only made me sad.

Stories from Goa kept us busy for a while before the bell greeted us with a new beginning.

Everyone scattered to their respective classes. I thought of skipping the classes, but then I went ahead to attend it. I was the only one studying business, rest were enrolled for different subjects.

Classes seemed like a nightmare, and I would often think about Viraj and Tseten who were in the same sociology class along with Dechen and Naina. Sumaira and Nadja were together in journalism, and I sat there waiting for our next round of madness together.

A month had passed by, and everything was moving as it was set to be . . .

Sanjeev walked into the cafeteria.

'There you are; I knew I could find you here. Rachel's sent you this.' He handed over a small package to me.

Before leaving, he reminded me of the upcoming gig. We were to start with our rehearsals starting the same day and had to stay back after the college hours.

Sanjeev then left . . .

I opened the pack, and it was a small note book. Inside, it was written 'Hope you will fill it up with your melodies someday.' (*Later, it became a vault that stored many of my songs that I wrote.*)

After the rehearsals, I headed home. Tired, I crashed into my bed; it wasn't up until late midnight, I woke up for a snack and went back to sleep again. Before I went back to sleep again, I sent an email to Rachel, thanking her for the lovely gift. I never heard back from her.

A week later, we had to perform in one of our neighbouring colleges, and it was there when I met Simran again. It was a pleasant surprise, and we were glad to see each other.

This time we exchanged our contact numbers and started texting.

As the stories in the cafeteria kept on building, the story with Simran was also being slowly outlined and was taking its own shape to a new painting.

I suddenly found myself close to her. Sharing daily events at the end of each day, it became a regular routine. Before time could tell, there were no secrets between us.

I don't know what was about Simran but hanging around her made me realise that I had so much to learn about the pureness of heart. Although an achiever herself, her heart was pure and innocent.

Music had connected us before, and as we got to know each other better, we realised we were identical copies of one another's soul—only trapped in a different form of energy. We believed and practised almost similar idea on life.

Nobody taught me that a friendship with a different energy form would require special protocols to be followed. Here I was, spending time with a friend who was exactly like me in every way but not just in the same form.

'Keep it simple,' I told myself then.

Simran and I had gone out for a coffee after we met again.

Dechen had dropped by later to be at the same café shop; she came alone.

Dechen was alone—no entourage with her? It was a refreshing moment.

Tseten and Naina also happened to be present and were seated at the next table. I was happy to see them around. I got them introduced to Simran. Dechen particularly was asking her with her endless questions.

The evening soon passed by, and it was time to head back home. After telling our goodbyes, Simran made her exit.

Dechen requested me to drop her on the way back, to which I humbly agreed. On the way, she told me that she had called it off with Jacob. It seemed distance was playing havoc with them, and both felt it was a torture for them to keep on dragging with their relationship.

Better wise than a fool tomorrow, they had mutually agreed to call it an end.

Dechen was happy to be single again; she realised how liberating it was to be out of a relationship.

Relationship, funny she was talking about it with me.

For the only thing that I understood was the picture we kept on drawing and how it kept on changing in time.

Relationship may be acquired through birth or by choice, but the picture around you, they keep on changing every single day.

How could one be sure about being liberated only after you have let go of someone or something?

Someone left you and now you are liberated?

(You know what I think? Stupid is what I think.)

Take a picture from your childhood and start in a chronological order. Your birth, first birthday, and so on, you will soon realise what I am talking about.

And even after looking at all your picture, if you don't understand, just ask yourself, how many people are leaving your life at this very moment?

'What would happen to you when you realise hundreds of them are departing from your life at this very moment? Look around carefully, many of them are silently fading away; it's just that we don't notice them. Time shall somehow remind you later.'

This is what was running in my head at that moment; before I could bring the dialogues in my mind to words, she asked the auto driver to stop and dropped off mid-way. I continued with my travel home. On the way, I thought about Dechen and what she had spoken.

If only I could have made Dechen understand life is made of 'arrivals and departures', and our job is only to find what we have finally taught our heart, I am sure she would have left smiling.

(But I guess sometimes, silence remains our biggest betrayal.)

Days and months had passed by, and we were approaching the last few days left together to spend with our college friends. Uncertainty rested our soul those days. Tseten and Viraj had plans to continue their further studies outside India once they were done with their graduation.

Dechen was all set for Sweden and had plans to join her uncle who had a small hotel business out there.

Simran was directed by her parents to relocate somewhere close to their home and wanted her to consider New Delhi as her new base. Whatever she wanted to do further had to be close to her parents' home.

Sumaira and Naina planned to head back to Nepal; their dad had a small IT firm and both wanted to help their dad grow his business bigger with their knowledge and skills learnt from a distant land.

About Nadja, there was no clue. We all assumed she would return to Germany post her graduation.

As for Adit, he had made it clear with his folks that he was staying back in Bangalore.

He had no intentions of going back to New Delhi to his parents' home and had plans that would help him win his extended stay in Bangalore.

He then enlightened me with his idea; it worked with Sir Major too. Mom never said anything . . .

(Adit and I had convinced our parents that we would complete our master's degree from the same city and to add more steel to our story, we stated that we would be studying together in the same college to help each other with studies.)

The air in the cafeteria had seen a sudden dip in the temperature those days. United Nations had grown silent with passage of time. There were members still having a year or two left with themselves to discover their own story in this very own circus, but they too were of less help in easing the situation and were helping their seniors to mourn their last few days left with everyone around.

(Everyone was helping each other to get sadder by reminding and counting the remaining days left at the college.)

Words such as *I already miss you, will miss you, remember me*, and *never forget*, blah! Blah! Blah! . . . were the greetings one could hear from most of the folks around. Girls went on an emotional crusade whenever the topic of the last remaining days in college erupted.

Whatever it is, I think it was the way of universe telling every one of us the importance of being present in the picture before the moment passed away.

(As for me, I quietly sat there, knowing this too would lead to something positive.)

And as it goes, the outcome of this long, cold winter would bring a fresh new plan for our grand exit. A final trip with all the friends to Goa—a place where everyone was eager to visit.

With this, the final days of our college arrived, and it brought in a long deserted days of hibernation to prepare for the final examination.

I remained at home mostly preparing for the upcoming papers. I knew the examination scores were the only way to keep myself safe from my parents' prying eyes. As long as my numbers were right and bright, I was safe from Sir Major's uncalled intervention.

(This was something that I never compromised; it was the price for my freedom that I could only earn.)

The day arrived when the pens felt, by far, the heaviest of weight carried so far.

Exams—Exams.

Before entering the examination hall, I met Tseten at the cafeteria; he was a bit nervous, and he mentioned that he was at the Brigade's the night before and was not prepared at all to write the examination.

I told him that the questions in his examinations would mostly come from the syllabus that had been covered in his class and should not hurt him much. I reassured him that he would surely recollect what was taught in the class.

Oh! I forgot.

Tseten was mostly at the cafeteria instead of his classroom.

He had managed to secure his hall tickets by paying a hefty penalty to the administration for not meeting his required attendance during his academic year.

He was still hung over from his previous night's spirit uplifting. He must have been drinking to overcome his examination fears.

I prayed for him and wished him luck.

The exams got over faster than I had thought it would take to get rid of.

But I would have to wait for others to complete their papers before we headed to Goa. A few of them still had their papers scheduled for a week later.

The day then arrived when all were done with testing our brains, and examination was over. What else? We were heading for Goa finally . . .

Dechen, Tseten, Naina, Sumaira, Viraj, Simran, Adit, and I were all geared up for the trip ahead and had gathered around the boarding point for the bus that would take us to Goa.

We had fifteen minutes before the bus left the depot. I climbed the bus and took the window seat next to the exit door. I saw Nadja seated right behind me. (Never knew she was joining us for the trip.)

Viraj took the seat next to me.

After an hour, the bus pulled over a roadside eatery for the passengers to take a quick bite. Everyone got down from the bus.

I wanted to remain inside and be with the music I was listening to.

I sat there singing along, thinking I was the only one in the bus.

It was only when someone had their hands on my shoulder from behind, I realised someone else was present in the bus too.

I turned to around to see Nadja smiling at me.

I was not aware that she was still there, only two of us in that bus, and Nadja smiling at me; though she had been different during the final year, looking at Nadja smile, I was petrified.

She laughed! She came and sat in the seat where Viraj was seated before. I wished her hello, and we both remained quiet for a while, before I was prodded by her.

I looked at her, she smiled again and said, 'Thank you.'

I was a bit confused, I asked her for what?

She mentioned it was for the friendship that I shared with her for the last three years. I smiled, and in that smile, she knew what it spoke. 'Everything was okay between us.'

Viraj was back after a quick fill and was carrying a bottle of cold drink mixed with the local spirit. I took a sip from it and offered it to Nadja. She thanked me and stated that she would better stay away from aerated drinks. She had some allergies to them. I promptly got the point and returned the bottle back to Viraj.

Nadja requested Viraj to take her seat and allow her to remain on the one that she was already seated then.

Viraj looked at me; though he tried not to give away anything, his expressions wore it all.

I looked at him while he slowly made his way behind.

Everyone settled, and the bus took off. I plugged the earphones back and silently slipped into the world of notes and melodies.

The night slowly grew heavy, and everyone had slipped into the world of dreams. For a while I thought half the folks in that bus would have already been dreaming about the music, party, beaches, sun, the sand, and the atmosphere in Goa . . . Party!

(Stories from my previous visit to Goa might have provided the required pictures to build their dream that night; for some, it might have been the power of new-age tool—they must have browsed to gather the required frame for their dream that night.)

One thing I am sure, every single soul in that group was dreaming about Goa that night, except for me. I smiled and turned only to see Nadja still awake.

'That makes two of us then?' I went on . . .

Nadja was amused; she did not understand what I meant.

I told her about my theory on the dreams our friends must have been dreaming the very moment, and how she was the only one not asleep and dreaming that night . . . She giggled!

She told me she found it funny.

I inquired why she was not yet asleep. She told me that she had never travelled on a bus before and had been struggling to get some sleep. I pulled the lever on her seat and brought the seat to recline.

Nadja quickly stretched her lazy self and said, 'This is so much better.'

She hurriedly wished me goodnight, and in no time, she entered her own dreamland.

I woke up with a funny smell. I realised we had hit the coastal line, and it was the nature's way of telling us that we were reaching our destination. Only on my return did I realise the smell was from a chemical factory that was located right outside the entrance of the city. I mistook it for the smell of fresh planktons washed away by the sea at night.

About half an hour later, we got down from the bus and took a taxi straight to Anjuna, where our accommodations had been arranged.

It was a nice two-storied building with stairs winding up to the top floor from inside the house. Fully furnished, it had four bedrooms, hall, and recreation area with a TV and music system on the first floor. Three of the bedrooms were at the top floor. Kitchen with oven and fridge, dining hall with tables and chairs, and the fourth bedroom was on the ground floor. It also had a green lush lawn in front of the house that overlooked the Arabian Sea. Perfect!

As everyone was busy settling down, I kept my luggage at the room and headed towards the waters. The beach was filled with shacks, and the shacks were filled with tourists that had travelled from all around the world.

I wished life was Goa always.

It was noon, and everyone was ready to explore the other parts of Goa and experience the insanity in it. We arrived at Vagator from Anjuna on the scooters we had hired for our exploration. We had five scooters; Naina rode pillion with Tseten, Sumaira took off with Viraj on his scooter, Dechen was asked to hitch a ride with Adit, and as for Simran, she tagged along with me.

Nadja took the scooter on her own as she knew how to ride one and had a valid motorcycle license with her. It was later in Vagator, I learnt from her that she had been riding since she was sixteen and her father had bought her own motorcycle when she had turned nineteen and she still had the bike at her garage back home.

Sorted with the business of our transportations, our stay in Goa had just commenced.

It must have been the stress of travelling overnight, everyone called it a day sooner than I had thought. At 10 p.m. every one of them was heavily breathing, and as for me? I was wide awake, with open eyes, staring at stars and lying down at the lawn that overlooked the Arabian Sea; I sat there thinking, what I had been thinking then.

'Can't sleep?'

I found Nadja standing next to me.

'Just came back from a walk in the beach, pretty dark out there, but it's beautiful,' she carried on.

I was surprised to see her up so late at night and had thought she too had retired for the day; she stood smiling and asked me to get up.

I reluctantly acknowledged her request. She then asked me to follow her. I followed her to the terrace. The view was much different from there; it radiated peace. The sea was shining silver as the moon smiled upon it. The clouds were playing a jealous bunch and shadowed the moonlight whenever it could.

But the night was drawing a picture to be framed in mind only. It was a picture unseen.

Nadja stood there still, looking at the end where the sea met the sky. The night was longing for a silent song. But the waves could not just master the rhythm in the air.

Heavy waves kept crashing on the shore line and every time they met, a thundering sound engulfed the air.

Nadja asked me to walk towards the edge of the terrace where she had been standing silent for a while. I told her it was not a good idea and suggested we sat down at the terrace itself.

She walked towards me and asked if the place I was standing was safe.

I sat down, and she followed suit. We sat there silent before we caught ourselves back into our reality and found it had been almost one at night.

We both knew the air between us had cleared itself, and the night had already grown tired.

We wished ourselves sweet goodnight and both retired to our own rooms.

The next day, we had a long ride towards Arambol Beach. The faces on the bikes were to be remembered; it was like an army of free souls gathered around to know life better.

Simran was riding pillion with me. I don't know what happened next and what made her move; all I can remember is after several brutal seconds of my life, I found myself lying on the ground; Simran, writhing in pain, was lying next to me.

When my eyes opened after a blip in a moment of my life, I was lying in a fancy hospital, with a cast on my hand and the other one holding the ice cream—given to me as a consolation prize.

Simran managed to escape with a brand-new set of bruises to flash.

After the accident, we mostly stuck around Anjuna, lazing on the beach and taking a quick dip in the Arabian Sea.

Yes, I watched it all the while it happened. My cast was prohibiting myself from causing any trauma to it and as advised by the men in the white coat, I had to take bed rest—*God must have also gone insane when he first said this word himself*—for a whole day.

You have no idea how much happens in a day. And missing a day in Goa is like years missed.

Whatever made Simran move while I was riding fine?

'Yeah, blame it on her, it might help end the guilt of being a victim,' my silent thoughts were riding high.

Tseten walked into the room and laughed at my very sight. He said that Simran was upset that I dropped her from the bike.

'Upset! She must be crazy. She was the one who moved because of which I could not control the scooter and ended up here,' I shouted.

Tseten could see the anxiety building in me, and he quickly used his wit to change the subject.

(It took a while, and I forgot what had happened.)

Towards the evening, the rest of the gang paid their visit. Simran wore a smile of an angel and quoted, 'Are you fine, Kabir?'

Nadja interrupted and shared the pictures from her camera; it was screaming stories from the day. Sadly, I was held up at the house from where I looked at them have fun.

It was time to break free with a fresh new dawn; the next day, I was on my way out from the nesting. With the cast still on, T still smelled good, as fresh from a laundry shop, I moved ahead of everyone and hiked my way to Vagator.

Had a sling bag hanging by my shoulder, inside which I had most of the required essentials to survive a day or two.

With the music on, the scenes slowly began to change.

Half way through my unknown destination, like a vagabond, my heart and soul walked a different route. This was a route unchartered by many souls.

I made my way to a brand-new journey for the mankind and reached a spot from where the water seemed a bit too close. A small man had made paths leading up the hill, which led to a trail to another world. It took me through a steep climb which was followed by a much gentle slope to negotiate while it came down to meet the shoreline. I arrived at a white sandy beach, only big enough to host not more than fifty people in it. It was a paradise that was hidden behind reality.

The realisation of being the only soul present at that lonely beach sent a chilling happiness inside. Here I was, one with the universe in me . . . .

The beach was hidden behind a steep mountain cliff; the greens around almost covered its presence from the normal human eyes. My soul sat there, unmoved, hours, looking at the clouds with the blue screen behind. My imaginations went wild, drawing up references as the clouds moved slowly through those screen.

The energy was positive, the air smelt a lot lighter in mood to greet anyone.

I was in the middle of a magical land with the two coconut trees that had grown side by side right in the middle of the pearly white beach; they appeared like a twin soul. It was as if paying a tribute to the picture of this wonderful magic land. Heaven, I remind myself again. I thanked the universe for allowing me to be where I was then.

After a soulful day at a place, colours soon faded away, and I was on my way back to a place where civilised were those who remained in pairs and groups—they called it reality.

I went back to share my adventure with the boys. The boys were looking forward to make this trip in time; just the four of us in a land where magic was the only reality.

'But how do we get rid of the girls?'

Great minds that work together, we all came by an excellent plan. We went back and told the girls that we would very much like them to remember their visit to Goa and to make it a memorable one for them—the gentlemen had decided to let them have an all-girls day out. They bought it.

The girls went running wild!

The next day, the guys packed with their required rations and, with their bags hanging behind, made their walk to the fairy land.

After a journey in space and in time, we finally reached our destination. Everyone was happy as hell.

That particular day, the sky went extra blue, the water reflected menthol green, and with friends whose hearts were singing along the same old melodies, there was an electric rush in the air.

Tseten was the poet in the group; he wrote his line out of air; words chosen carefully, he made his point all clear. The flow of his words lightened up the mood to insanity.

Adit was almost uncontrollable with his jokes; it kept on flooding the space all the time. We all laughed like mad men.

Viraj had tagged his guitar along and sang his beautiful songs as the day ended. I still remember him sing 'Green

Fairy' song and while the beautiful sun hid behind a crimson sky, the moon was still playing hide-and-seek.

Tseten wrote a beautiful line that day. If I recall it correctly, it went somewhat like this:

In our heart, we are but one;

Divided we remain, only in our thoughts.

Such is the beauty of this universe;

Thank you for the reminder, why together we were all brought.

That day, I learnt something new about Viraj, something that changed our friendship only to last forever. Viraj and I had been friends for almost three years, and we used to share stories with each other but never the one like that day.

We had found a brief moment to ourselves while Adit and Tseten had ventured into the greens. He narrated his life to me.

Silently, I listened to him and thought, 'We were so different in what we understood of life, yet here we were together as friends, understanding what the other had to say.'

I thought I already knew a lot about Viraj and thought he had shared quite a deal with me on his life. He had spoken about his girlfriend, and how he considered her as one of the pillars of his life. He always said his girlfriend and his aunt were the two pillars of his life. He never spoke much about his parents and of any other folks from his past.

But that day, he spoke in length about his life; that day, he shared me a picture from his life, much personal and close to him.

I learnt both his parents were killed in a road accident. Viraj was only five-year-old then. His mom's sister had taken over the responsibility of grooming him into becoming a man. He spoke about his aunt and the sacrifice she had made in her life for him. How she was working as a housekeeper in a hotel in Singapore just to raise and provide a proper education for him.

He had been in the boarding's his entire life, mostly spending his time there. If he was lucky, he would meet his aunt once in a year; at times, it would turn to be two.

He shared his one single dream with me; he wanted to complete his studies as soon as possible to pursue his dream of getting his aunt back to Nepal, have a decent job and a place to stay as a family, along with the love of his life.

I don't know why he shared with me such personal information. But I instantly realised that he trusted me, just like his own brother.

That day I thanked my stars to have brought me friends like the ones I had around. They became my family.

It was about ten at night; we finally reached back to our base. The girls had not yet returned. We waited for them, talking about the green fairy-tale adventure.

It was our last day in Goa, and we had a bus to catch for Bangalore that evening. With all the hired scooters returned, we spent the day lounging at the beach in Anjuna. With waves running high, the sun making its presence felt by its rays that could roast a chicken alive, my lazy little soul remained silent, lying on the hammock shaded by the leafy green of the coconut trees that suspended the hammock mid-air. My universe was within me.

(Only for a brief moment I was interrupted by the thoughts of a falling coconut from up above—mostly I was left alone at peace.)

Nadja walked to me; she had the usual smile that she had acquired during the final days. I was in no mood to entertain anyone, yet I was somehow dragged out of my universe and was found readying for a dash to the forest for a quick hike. I really don't know how she did it.

It was during this moment, she told me that the first two years of her anger towards me was a misplaced one. She told me that I reminded her of her past, the one that she had left behind. I guess it was something about the way I was that reminded her of him.

I don't know whatever it meant, but she was being honest then.

With my mouth slightly open, no signs of breathing or any movement on my face, I listened to her speak.

With the passing of time, it seems she had realised that I was a complete different person. So what a few of my personality was a definite match with her past? When she realised there were other shades to me, she wanted to call it a truce and become friends.

I told her I thought we were already friends. She smiled.

With everyone on board, the bus to Bangalore started its engine and roared its way through the highway.

Bangalore again, and the day came by for everyone to exchange their contact information and to say their goodbyes.

Everyone left Bangalore.

Adit and I were the only ones left behind.

Unknown of what was in front of us, life quickly moved us into another frame.

5

The next two years went by a flash. These two years, most of us were in touch with each other in some way or another. We kept ourselves updated with the news on the developments of each other's life.

But sometimes, time can eat you alive. You disappear from the picture, and you find yourself busy describing the pictures that were there before. Surely we don't realise the new pictures are still being painted around.

Memories make a fool out of you.

In those two years, Adit and I went attending an evening college pursuing our higher degree.

MBA, isn't it what everyone wants to do these days?

Well, that was the only other option provided to me by Sir Major, else I had to get myself enrolled to the uniform.

I dreaded being like him; since childhood I had a terrible relation with discipline. I would rather stick around with a heap of books, rather than be lectured on how I am to be.

I suggested Sir Major, MBA would surely help me in getting an edge with my application to the uniform— whenever that was to happen.

He slept over it for several months and had finally signed it off, only just in time before I was to return.

But for me, I was already telling everyone that I was to remain in Bangalore.

Maybe Adit staying back and pursuing MBA also helped.

Whatever, here I was still amusing myself with every single explanations of life.

Funny, how life's dramas to unfold, we only have to wait for time to tick by.

The college Adit and I got the master's degree from was not too keen on maintaining a comprehensive track record on their students' attendance and, with this added benefit, both Adit and I kept ourselves at a safe distance from it.

One fine day, I don't know what went inside Adit's head, he wanted to attend classes and made me come along.

We were seated at the last desk of the class and paid attention only to our own chats. That day the classes got over around eight, and we made a dash towards Brigade.

(It was time to catch up with a decent meal and then head straight to the theatre to accommodate the last show of the day.)

That night we also reached home a little different. You know what I mean?

Slightly uplifted spirits from Bangalore's finest.

We had managed to sneak in sometime to visit a pub in-between the movie and the meal.

The next day was repentance; Adit woke up with an upset stomach, and I woke up seeing two Adits. What a waste! Neither of us could recollect the movie we both watched that night.

Am I forgetting something?

Oh yes! Forgot, we met Vignesh in our class that day. Later that night, he had joined us in our expedition.

Vignesh Naidu was a young, confident, and a brilliant fellow, born and brought up by a father who was one of the famous businessmen in the country. The air of being as the son of such a recognised individual could not be traced in him.

But he was someone who could not miss your sight. Must have been his privileges to unwanted flavours of life, this boy wore brand all over him. He could stand out in the crowd, and by just looking at the dress, you would know it was him.

Well, we all started hanging around for a while, mostly at my place. Vignesh used to miss his class to pay his attendance at ours. Time rolled by, and it was during this phase, I got to know that he had been seeing Sunaina.

We were so used to calling her Naina, it never struck us before, the stories he was sharing about his girlfriend Sunaina was none other than our own Naina.

It was only when he later spoke about the college she attended; Good Lord did Adit and I realise Naina had been seeing Vignesh as well, exactly the same time she was with Tseten.

He also updated us that they had intentions of getting married which went sour because of her decision to return.

Adit went asking for more details on their relationship. I don't know what I was doing then, but I remained thinking and was in a world unknown to me before.

Music had been slowly dying away from my life; the circles that moved along had been moved somewhere far away from my reach, and it had seemed it had been scattered all around.

Adit was preparing his return to his parents' home.

From college to higher degree, Adit's presence had been constant in my life. And here he was about to leave me behind.

Growing up without a sibling, there was always a need to have a brother or a sister with whom you could share your little mischief, pranks, and a bit of trouble too. He was that to me.

(Not that I never had my share of fun, I had madness around me, but they had always been with my friends.)

Adit was in my life for the last five years sharing these shenanigans, but he was my brother, we shared the blood.

So what even if it was just the half of it running in me, it was different thrill having our little share of mischief. Always learning something new, nothing stopped us from painting our own picture to remember.

(I always knew Adit was running away from something, from what? I had no clue. But deep down, I had the faith that he would share it with me what he had to, only when the time was right.)

Our life had been a circus, only medicine available was to laugh and forget. What he was about to share before he left, changed something in me, if not entirely.

He said that day, that he was hiding away from love, the love that suffocates. With that, he spoke everything about his reality.

He had grown up just fine, but his parents had never taken him seriously and considered him an adult. For them he was still the little Adit who knew nothing about the evil world and had to be guided around.

As for Adit, he wanted to find life on his own.

It must have been the blood in him which gave him the thirst to learn more about life; just like me, he too was running from something he never understood.

He was running away trying to find himself in the madness of this reality, the reality of life.

Adit was running away from love and as for me?

As you know, I was a free soul running away from so-called self-control imposed by what others believed and was always finding for myself, what my heart is to be.

The day arrived when Adit took on a different journey.

By now, Sir Major had realised my intentions 'loud and clear' and, with many bruises to his ego, gave his nod. I was to stay back and pursue my dreams in Bangalore.

How did I do it?

Well, I shared with him the appointment letter to an esteemed organisation, which I had managed to secure through the campus recruitment. The last section of the letter might have blown Sir Major's mind. He never challenged my thoughts.

But the truth is, I never took up the job that had made Sir Major's change his mind. Instead, I got back with music, and this time, it helped me survive.

And guess what? I was making twice of what was quoted in the appointment letter that had blown Sir Major Brains away, and what more could I ask for? It came with an added benefit with parties to attend.

I made enough to enjoy an excellent living in a city best known as one the most expensive to survive. I was proud of myself.

The universe had always been with me. There I was playing gigs at parties, celebrations, anniversaries, weddings, shows, and festivals and making money together with my best friend.

(While she went screaming my heart with the music that poured out of her lungs, I was narrating the messages for the mass through her.)

I was doing all this to secure my freedom and to find my own understanding of reality. Who cares!

Sir Major must have thought, 'So what if my son does not wear a uniform, he wore a tie at least.'

But I was living the moment in whatever I could fit in. As for my parents, they were not aware where their son had arrived.

I moved into my own apartment, and it must have been sometime that I had finally found a place to call my home.

I loved the evenings at the balcony, watching birds taking their final round of flight, guided by the fading sunlight, and the small paddle boats still awaiting its return. Bangalore was truly the garden city of mine.

(The story of life now was slightly different. Now the picture had changed completely. Though the stories of arrivals and the departures were still there in the subject, only the conditions to it had changed.

Frequent short visits from friends, business or personal, were ensured by a must catch-up moments. In schools, we used to catch up in minutes and hours; in colleges, in days and weeks; and now the time had moved to months and years before we even said hello.)

Time comes in life when faces around you will be fairly new; it was one of those moments of my life. Every day, there were different energies floating around, and the insanity in it had slowly started to overwhelm me. I got caught with life, that's what I said then.

Life, such a big word to use so casually, who knew then?

Anyway, it was the time when madness in me had reached its peak. Travel became my second best friend. The first one you know her, right? (Guitar)

It was the moment when I learnt that my entire life, I had learnt nothing and had to unlearn everything I had learnt so far.

There was so much to explore, so much to discover, and there I was stupidly thinking that I had seen it all.

It was a déjà vu.

'I have not learnt anything yet? I think I have felt this same before. Stop it!' I told my curious mind.

I started accepting more and more events that would take me to new places, meet fresh faces, new ideas, new thoughts, their likes and dislikes. Life had become a map that I wanted to explore for myself; it had turned even bigger this time.

It was in one of those trips to Delhi, I met Tseten after a long haul.

Too bad it was just a brief reunion with him; I had to head back to Bangalore the very next day.

I could see grief in his eyes; good old friends from good old days, and there we were, meeting in an unknown city, and time was what we were fighting against.

How come everything got suddenly changed, and the canvas had been cleaned white with him as well? I couldn't even pull up a single reference to draw the picture that we used to create before.

Don't take it wrong. We were the same as before, but the picture that was getting sketched at that very moment—something was wrong on it.

Why? I don't know.

It must have been the time? We both didn't have like the good old days. We both knew we wanted to share more moments of madness like before; but both knew that there was no point to it. We did not have time to complete our stories; we chose not to touch topics that would stretch to nothing.

We just spoke about the good old days and then headed in our own direction.

(Sad, could not meet Adit during that trip; he had gone for a tour to Himachal with his friends.)

I was on my way to the exit at the airport; I heard a loud shout, 'Kabir!'

I turned around to the direction it came from.

I recognised the voice. Just to be sure enough, I needed to catch a glimpse of her. There she was standing brighter than the sun that day. It must have been due to the colour of the top that she wore that particular day—blushing pink; it made her skin appear radiant than lights that filled the day.

What can I tell you about Nisha? She's insane.

She had come all the way to airport to pick me up. She was one of the few close friends I was left with in that time.

She was always high on life and cared a wind to none. We met during one of my shows. Initially, I had found her a little too proud. It was only when we met for the second time during her parents' anniversary party, where I was to perform, we bonded better and knew we were friends that were just waiting to get introduced by time.

You see she was the perfect person in my life at that point of time. We were both not confined by the rules laid by the crowd.

So what, I had learnt to handle them with care by now.

As for what rest of the world thought? They thought what they thought it to be. We were busy finding happiness in what we were doing then.

Three of us went spinning hysteria in the air.

Oh yes, other regular character in my life then was her elder brother, Udhav. Three of us were always found in every part of the city, loafing our time away and painting fresh new memory.

My job gave me the flexibility to experience life in its much better form.

Just because the crowd demanded, I saw a lot of folks take up so-called white-collared job and meet needs way above their skills. I also saw the same folks chewing their own words and feasting on air at times. They were busy making their bank accounts fatter, and as their bank account grew fatter and bigger, their heart grew smaller every single day.

I thanked God for giving me the gift of appreciating myself.

Udhav and Nisha were renowned fashion designers by profession and had a boutique at Richmond Town.

They had just finished a clothing line which was to be released in the upcoming month and had arranged a small get-together to kick-start the promotional work. They had invited some of their close and influential acquaintances to get some timely leads for their business.

It was time for a party at their place, and I had to be a part of it.

Life had entered a different frame with all the souls disappearing faster than the speed of sound. 'Hello, I could hear, but where was the goodbye?'

I found it safe being around Nisha and Udhav, two good souls who were from the same city and were the faces that regularly greeted me.

Funny now when I think hard, Sanjeev was still around but meeting him had been ages.

I am sure we might have crossed our paths on several occasion, just that we might have had changed so much that we might have not recognise one another.

'Well, is that possible?' *It could have been the case.*

Guests started flooding, and the evening had just begun. The place was swarming with faces that were only seen at that moment.

Udhav and Nisha, being the host, were busy tending the guests. I remained at the corner of their balcony and watched the moon silently wink at the sky.

Moments later, a gentleman stood next to me, holding his drink steady as he quoted,

'If moon would have some shame in her, she wouldn't act too proud on her borrowed beauty.'

I turned around to find a better view of him; there he stood in a black suit, sporting white hair; he must have been nearing his fifties, but he surely maintained his health to look forever young. It might have only been his hair that gave away his age; else it would have been a puzzle for any to put a guess around his age.

He introduced himself as Mr Pankaj Naren; he was into entertainment business. I listened to him speak for a while before I was distracted by Udhav who had been requesting me to dish out some new melodies to turn the evening alive.

I took his guitar and sang my merry songs.

Soon, everyone got together and started to follow. It was a night when my life would take a sudden jump.

It turns out that Mr Pankaj Naren was into some event-management business and had several contacts and was looking out for someone exactly like me. In his own words, a talent undiscovered.

He had a proposal; he was willing to promote my music and produce my first album. All I had to do was to sign a two-year contract with him.

He told me it included music tours that would not be more than one or two major shows at any given month. Percentage of the profit was to be shared from the sales of the music albums and from the events that I attend.

(What else am I forgetting?)

Oh yes!

He was offering me an insane amount of money as the signing bonus, what more?

I went ahead and signed.

My dream to reach out to a larger audience and to share my paintings, drawn with the help of the musical notes—time had finally arrived.

Months-long rehearsals took away my time before the actual recording was completed. Days and nights were spent editing the songs. It was a long wait before the final master record was approved. The creative team sat hours over the weekends, drawing up ideas for the album cover.

Mr Naren was in no mood to compromise with the quality of the work that would be finally presented to the end consumer. The moments were building quickly, and the time for the release date was approaching fast.

In our final hours, we were still discussing the picture that would be printed on the album cover. And we were still fighting over the topics for the picture that would represent the music inside.

A sudden flash and I shouted, 'Thoughts that betrays my brain.'

'Perfect!' said Mr Naren. 'Talks volumes of what your music says. Do you also have any thoughts on what would be the picture to describe your message to go with the album cover?'

I told him, it should be plain white with just those words written on it, right in the middle.

The album went on to break a new record.

I became someone everybody thought they knew something about, and it happened overnight—as soon as the albums got released.

The reports of the success story of my new album reached far across the world. Suddenly, everyone got interested in knowing more about me.

While the new faces got closer to know more on me, the old ones were rapidly disappearing from the frame.

I was struggling to reach out to my old pals, but 'time' was the only luxury I never had then.

Everything around me was changing at a pace I had never experienced before.

Time had exploded itself. It was racing beyond my imagination.

After the release of the album, about a month, my life remained untouched.

I did a few gigs around promoting the music. The energy level had been the same till then.

Time and again, Mr Naren would call me up to give an update on the sales figures and would congratulate me on my newfound success.

In-between I had gone to visit my parents for some time. Mom told me that she was thrilled to see me on TV and spoke about the news programme where she had seen me answering questions.

Dad had gone out when I reached my parents' home. Later in the evening, he walked in, he saw me chatting with mom at the dining hall, and he walked right into his room. Mom told me not to worry, and everything would be fine. She went to the room where Dad had locked himself, and after a while, she walked back with him.

Dad told me that he was fine when I told him that I was not joining the army and taking up the job with the multinationals that were paying me insane amount of money. But the fact that I had hidden the reality from them hurt him a lot.

This sudden surprise had shocked him.

He said that he would have understood if I had told him once and if only had I shared with them what I wanted from my life, they would have understood.

But, I know, they would have never understood my pain had I shared my thoughts with them. They would have clipped my wings and ensured I followed theirs instead, as I was their only hope to continue their legacy.

I was surprised to see my dad who had always been the tough army guy, sitting broken in front of me. I don't know if it was his 'ego' that was hurt, or he must have realised something deeper, but that day I found my dad to be a different man.

We sat and had our dinner together that night, sharing stories of our good time. Mom kept asking me to extend my stay, but a week's time was all that I got to spend with them.

Back to Bangalore from this short visit to my parents, Mr Naren came by my place later in that evening. He sat for a while and had a drink to warm his soul and informed me that we were running booked up until next one year.

It sounded like fun. There were shows that were scheduled all over the country. Sometimes we performed at one place and took a flight directly to another and performed at our next venue the very next day.

Life was a merry-go-round, and I was getting lesser and lesser time to spend at my Bangalore house.

With my newfound access to free-flowing fund, I had bought the same house that I was staying in from the previous owner from whom I had rented it.

He charged me double, I know for sure, but my soul wanted to rest in that same place for some more time. The place spoke a lot about me in this crazy world.

The only constant face around me those days had been Mr Naren. He was managing all my business-related affairs, while all I had to do was share the messages through my guitar. Mr Naren had become my genie. All I had to do was wish.

Anything I wanted and Mr Naren would weave his magic to make it appear right in front of my eyes.

Life became a piece of cake, and I was feasting on it.

The media were a silly bunch. They ran the same questions again and again during the interviews.

Instead of talking about my work, they were interested in where I had been. The story of my life is what they wanted to know, and they kept repeating the same. I was growing tired with my explanations and went on a silent way.

The media made a story on that too. Guess they were just trying to cash in with their newfound scapegoat in me. The more information they were able to collect on me, the better their gossips were selling.

In this glare, I could hardly be myself. I was slowly becoming what they wanted me to turn into. I had not realised it then.

The further I was trying to run from the things that I used to keep my distance from; the closer they appeared to be.

Constant realisation of your life not being your own starts the time ticking, ticking for it to explode.

I always used to be in control of the person I am, what has happened to me now? What has changed?

This was the feeling that had begun slowing down my life.

What if I had run or walked a little faster? I guess that too would have been of no good.

I had started to feel I have been running forever. Running behind something that I needed to find on my own, but my life had turned out to be different from what I had thought it would turn out to be.

Even for a toothbrush, I had to ask Mr Naren to have them arranged. I was always busy doing something else.

Mostly, performing at the shows or busy shuttling in-between cities or partying around . . . I had been racing time.

Is this what I had signed up for?

You see, doing the same thing again and again, it dries you up slowly but steadily, until one moment it catches you by surprise.

Then your life is caught in a fast-moving paralysis, and it sits right down in front of you; you think hard and freeze your heart—nothing comes up to your brains. Then you do nothing but let time do what it has to do . . . You wait.

Almost a year of the same routine had drained me of my life. Hate drank me alive, and all I wanted was to be out of the web I had created around myself; no more of it for some time.

I loved music and would do anything for it. But I was literally being dragged, almost every day to make money for the people with whom I had signed a lawful paper called contract. And failing to honour as the crowd says would lead to serious consequences.

Mr Naren was a businessman first, simple as that. Everything he was came after it, and trust me, I had seen him sue some of the individuals buck naked, just because they had failed to honour Mr Naren's will.

The same place that I loved the most at one point of my life, I was found inching myself to get back in.

Mr Naren, though he wanted me to be a fine artist, highly recognised for my contributions towards the field of art, but he was a businessman in his heart first.

I have to be real honest, he never interfered with my creative work; but when it came to the finances, he was a bit overzealous character and signed deals that would send me travel crazy.

Sometimes I had to travel without sleep and perform straight shows. Then take a flight or a cab to reach another destination.

I was made to catch up with sleep while on the run and then I would find myself back on stage—performing.

All the while, he had been telling me that these entire craze was required for me to reach where they believed I should be. I believed him.

Initially I had fun with this sudden change. But as and when time grew by, I don't know what might have changed to feel the way I felt; life had started to grow much heavier on me.

Mr Naren came to my house after the end of the monsoon festival and informed me about the show he had signed off, scheduled a week later in Kathmandu—Nepal.

I was to perform in the annual international music festival held every year in the small Himalayan kingdom.

Initially, I resented the idea, it would require me to travel several thousand kilometres, and I had just returned from an international assignment. My bones wanted to chill.

It didn't matter even if the travel was by air. It was too far for me to accommodate in such a short notice. I informed him the same.

But then again, Mr Naren went on convincing that the money in this deal was running high, and he did not want this opportunity to be missed. He promised to keep my calendar free for a month as soon as we were done with our planned commitments. I happily agreed.

We reached Delhi airport around ten in the morning. The early flight from Bangalore had left me with very little sleep. The air around me was blurry, and the atmosphere was buzzed by the regular announcements of the arrival and departures of the birds.

We would have to wait for another three hours before our flight departed to the Himalayan town in a country residing locked behind the nature's highest wall.

We were at the airport lounge and waiting for our connecting flight, and most of the crew members along with Mr Naren sat right at the corner of the lounge—indulging with their desired poison.

I was thinking of my last visit to Kathmandu, which happened during my boarding days. One of my classmates' parents was kind enough to take me for a tour on their son's request. Somehow they had convinced Sir Major to approve my vacation.

Every picture from the memory was flashing back at a speed of the light, and I was eager to set my foot in the Himalayas again.

The boarding announcement was finally made, and the passengers were asked to proceed towards the designated flight. We all left towards the boarding gate as directed. As I made my way towards the boarding gate, a pleasant surprise caught me by. I was glad to see Viraj standing in the queue. He was in the same flight that was bound to Kathmandu.

I shouted aloud calling his name and trying to grab his attention. Viraj turned around and looked at me carefully. It took him a moment before he could figure it was me. We both were happy to see each other. I shared him with the details on my Kathmandu visit; we both promised to meet up and exchanged our contact numbers before proceeding towards the aircraft.

About an hour long journey, and we landed at the capital city of Nepal.

I met Viraj once again at the Kathmandu airport. It was then I learnt from him post his higher studies in States, he had returned to Nepal and had ventured into a small business. He had married his childhood love a year back, and they now stayed with his aunt who was back in Kathmandu.

Before we parted, we promised to catch up again. *Free from time telling us where we need to be next—we were to meet.*

With that promise the next day was followed by the show in which I had to perform. I saw Viraj backstage.

He made it, and I was happy to see him. His wife had also come along, and there was someone else with them as well.

Sumaira was standing right behind them.

I asked Mr Naren to take care of them while I went on with my job. The night was young, and the crowd?

Words would fail to describe them; they must have been born singing.

They knew what I was there for.

I loved my audience, and I thanked my God.

After I was done on stage, I hurriedly went towards the backstage to meet Viraj and Sumaira. It had been ages since we had shared a moment together, and it was as if the universe telling us—go lose yourself to the drawings that had been left incomplete years ago.

Catching up with old friends somehow is a moment that has always reminded me of my favourite sitcoms.

Imagine yourself religiously following TV soap for some time, until something comes along and you forget about the story for a blip—blip in your own time in space. Though the blip might have been only for a few seconds, it somehow converts itself into eternity. And finally when the blip disappears and you get back with the story to continue and find yourself back in front of the idiot box, you find the story needs some time to settle down.

There we were, good old friends, though the known faces around visibly shrunk in numbers, we were still glad to see each other.

Sumaira updated me that she was still helping her dad with his business, and it had picked up some speed in moving towards the direction she had always envisioned. She was also with the same guy she had been with in college, and they had their intentions to tie the knot by that mid year.

I congratulated her and wished her luck for her future.

As for Naina, she had carried on with her life and had been married for three years to a gentleman she had met in Kathmandu after her return from Bangalore.

Sumaira told me that Naina too wanted to meet me, but she had been visiting her in-laws several hundred miles away. She could not make it.

I extended my stay in Kathmandu by another week and got my return tickets redone. Mr Naren was a bit worried with my decision.

(He must have thought it was a little too longer than he had expected. But he had nothing to bring up as an excuse to drag me along with him. The next show I was to perform had been cancelled due to some technical disagreement with the sponsors.)

Rest of the commitments lined up until the next major one were all charity events and was not pinching Mr Naren's wallet. He was forced to cancel it on my request.

That gave me two free weeks before I was to be back on stage.

Mr Naren left Kathmandu; I went to stay with Viraj until my return. Viraj's family made me feel a part of them. I could be me all the while and his aunt was a lady filled with grace and his wife was a sister that I had never had. I was comfortably at home.

How, I missed being home. The hotel had become a place I always found myself in.

Time spent in Kathmandu, Nepal, was time well spent. To my surprise, even Tseten made it while I was in Kathmandu.

Viraj had informed Tseten about my visit to Kathmandu and had asked Tseten to come over, and he had made it there just in time.

The four of us got together and celebrated the moment of togetherness with insanity, flowing around once again.

On my way to Bangalore from Kathmandu, I had a connecting flight to catch from New Delhi, which meant another long waiting hours at the Delhi airport.

I was getting a little bored as I was travelling alone. I looked inside my bag to find anything that would help me save my moments; the music players had run out of its juice, and it was same with the phone.

I took out the laptop. It lasted fifteen minutes before it started to go epileptic on me.

I decide to take a tour of the market that had been stylishly set up inside the waiting area of the airport. I looked at my watch, and it still showed I had another two hours before I could proceed towards the boarding gates. I started to browse through the items that had been kept at display.

Even before I could look at some of them, the sales individual quickly suggested the items they had for display were custom exported and were exquisite and highly expensive. I don't know what he was trying to suggest, but he was clearly suggesting that the products in their shops were of no interest to me, and I was simply wasting both of our time, just by being there.

I never had such an experience before? *Well, Mr Naren always got me what I needed.*

'How come I have become so dependent?'

Anyway, my Image of a carefree soul is what the majority had always failed to understand.

I had always met this world as a friend. No judgement in this universe; I always believed time will tell you everything. And there I was, being judged for who I was then. I could have afforded to buy his entire store if I had wished to, but I chose to walk away in silence.

Too bad, I had every intention to pick up something from that place.

But then, it was his loss, I reminded myself.

I moved myself to the restaurant and got myself something to hang around with. I sat with it until the boarding of the flight to Bangalore was finally announced.

I reached Bangalore late that night. When I opened the doors to my apartment and as I turned the lights on, my universe slowly started to come back to me.

I slept at peace again.

The next day arrived early from an early morning call that broke my chain of dreams; it was Mr Naren.

He wanted to check if I was back.

God knows why Mr Naren was so paranoid about me.

We both agreed to meet up at twelve at a joint that served breakfast the entire day.

Later that noon, I met Mr Naren at the same joint and had a wholesome lazy Sunday breakfast. Mr Naren declined to have anything as he had his fast on.

I never noticed he was a religious person inside; he always looked more of an atheist to me. *Funny!*

He wanted to discuss on the contract which was about to get exhausted in the coming month. He wanted to be sure that I would be continuing my work with him.

I told him that I was not in a mood to talk about it then. I reminded him, deep down, he already knew my answer. I could see a sense of relief in him.

He insisted on clearing the bill; I thanked him and went to meet Udhav and Nisha in the evening.

On my way, I called Udhav to check if they had reached the venue where we were supposed to meet. As usual, they were running late. They promised to reach the venue in an hour's time. They had just started from their place.

So that was another two hours from the said time.

Always remember to add an hour to your actual travel minutes whenever travelling in Bangalore.

That is exactly how long it takes to reach anywhere with the traffic on.

Never believe in what people tell you, they can tell you a lot.

Anyway, they reached exactly two hours from the time I last spoke to Udhav. Till then, I had been exploring around.

It had been ages I had visited that part of the city. Many changes were painted to it, and it was shimmering like 'Vegas'.

Those two kind souls had already booked a table for us at the top section of the liquor garden we were to meet. The menu filled with paradox, boasted about the world's finest to present.

There was an upcoming band that was performing that night. I followed their music and sat silently observing the unknown faces only grow in numbers and crowd the place. The time slowly ticked away.

We stayed there until eleven, before we found our way back to my home. The story continues . . .

Udhav and Nisha complained about my sudden disappearance from their life those days, and how the regular meets were becoming events forgotten.

I told them I was busy with life. Whatever it meant?

But they seemed to understand that I was only doing what life demanded from most of us—to survive.

How wrong of them to think I was here just to survive, I was here to feel the change and was after the final message which seemed to elude my reality—forever.

Why bother them with the technicality of life? I reminded to quiet my thoughts.

We sat chatting along with the souvenirs that we had brought along from liquor garden to my apartment.

It was late morning when Nisha finally gave to her sleepy eyes and started to annoy Udhav by repeatedly asking him to say his goodbye.

Udhav, on the other hand, wanted to stay a little longer to share what he had in his mind.

Thanks to Nisha, I retired to my dreams after they left.

Short brief meets with known faces around had now given me the boost to take a bigger leap in my life. I got even busier and kept pushing my limits and started losing behind the track of time. I made a journey again, this time alone.

At that moment of my life, I shared a different relationship with guitar. I had started to hate her company, and travel had taken over her.

I was sharing her company only because it provided me the opportunity to be with travel.

Travel took me to a brand-new frame. The buildings, the roads, the ambience, it all started to build new sketches in my life, rather than the sketches drawn by human faces.

I loved the fact it got me introduced again with the mountains that I was so much in love with.

Not just the mountains, but it took me to deserts, beaches, and everywhere.

Travel was a friend who made me meet everyone, unlike Guitar, who only spoke what I had in my mind. Travel, she was different.

She made me understand that sometimes being a part of a bigger picture itself is a gift to realise.

The more I travelled, the lesser the faces started to appear and in the frames.

Time had skipped a long interval.

It made me meet intellects on the way; they taught me how to train my mind.

(The royalties, they taught me about grace; the ones in need, they taught me about humility; and the proud ones taught me how to care.)

How I had to learn about life? No subjects can cover the learnings of life . . .

But the truth is? I was still learning, lessons were not over yet.

There are long hours to go even before we have finished completing the introduction on the subject of life, we can only wait for our end to arrive.

Travel always brought a smile upon my face. Without her in my life, I started feeling a little out of air.

Guitar remained mostly away from me, unless it had to help me buy my needs.

Though after a while I had comparatively slowed down a bit with my madness with travel, she remained my best friend then.

'Guitar, I am not sure what had become of us.'

Whenever travel and I were apart, I mostly shared time with Udhav and Nisha. Their request for me to turn the evenings in harmony would fall in a deaf ear as it would require for me to be with Guitar. I didn't want to indulge with it then.

(Nisha must have felt sorry for her, as one fine day, she gave it a try to make friends with Guitar. The biting words from Udhav in a form of sarcasm might have forced her to reconsider her intentions.

They did not understand each other. She finally walked away from her.)

That day I learnt something new, it was not the Guitar's fault; it was me. I was the one who had taught her only to share my thought, and there she was refusing to say what Nisha had to share.

I know she would talk to my heart and scream my dreams. She was still the same.

So what happened? Why did I hate her then?

It was me who had changed. I was trapped in a world that was created by myself. *Little could I do with the realisation back then.*

Things had started to change better after my newfound enlightenment. I was back with travel; this time, I brought along Guitar wherever I went. Travel she never got jealous of her.

But in time, the glare from the constant attention from the crowd had almost blinded me. I stood there in my own world, everything was pitched dark and empty everywhere I looked around myself.

The spotlight was hiding away everyone.

I was following my own rules, my own imagination to navigate through the path in time.

I told myself, I was learning something new.

While Guitar and Travel had become my constant company, I forgot there were forces conspiring against our friendship silently.

It had been a few days since I had my contract renewed with Mr Naren. I had agreed to continue working with him for another year.

Guess what, Mr Naren was not happy with my decision, the last one was two, he grumbled.

By now, you must be aware that music had been my passion, and I had signed up to share it with everyone. But the previous experience was a bit edgy; hence, I wanted to go slow and sign off risks well before.

A year to me did not sound as bad as it did for Mr Naren, who had been negotiating an additional year. He was unhappy when I stuck to one year only commitment and refused his proposal for another two-year contract.

I was not running away anywhere and had signed a year deal, only to ensure that I was not lost again.

With Guitar and Travel slowly getting along perfectly together, I wanted to take it a slow.

I made this clear to Mr Naren, who finally acknowledged what I had to say.

The new season began, and Mr Naren was still my genie. He kept waving his magic wand and got me everything that I wanted.

Life was still a piece of cake.

But, it was oblivious of the reality that it had been growing heavy on Mr Naren.

The pressure of making more from the short opportunity was gradually building upon him. He only had a year this time to collect as much as he could.

He feared I would not continue working with him further.

'Who can treat a mind already filled with thoughts?'

But those were the exact ones running in Mr Naren's head.

I suddenly felt a huge change in the energy around; it was a sudden change in energy—the ones that come and deplete you.

Initial months went as it used to be. It was only after a couple of months later, I felt the sudden rush.

I had three shows lined up in Delhi the same day. 'Must have been a mistake. It is okay, no big deal,' I told myself and went on finishing it in style.

The crowd still loved me.

After Delhi, I was to travel straight to Chandigarh. A day off and then had two venues to attend and perform. I still thought Mr Naren might have smartly worked it out so that I could work at a stretch and take some time off before I got back on stage.

After the events were completed in northern part of India, I found myself free for a week. I was back at my Bangalore home.

Not knowing what to do for the rest of the free days ahead, I took out my bike and went for a ride.

Destination still not decided in my mind, but the tires had already burned the roads and left its mark.

I headed towards the northern part of Karnataka. Solo, with the winds hitting my hair; while the helmet that was to shield me from danger hanging by the rear-view mirror, the bullet slowly thumped its way, far away from the noise that made its heartbeats drown.

Soon the darkness took charge of the world, and my mind grew quiet as I hit the road with the beams flashing from another good friend—my motorcycle. He silently made his presence felt with his thumping sound.

My mind settled—Gokarna was the place where I was headed.

I had learnt about this place from a fellow traveller I had met in Delhi years ago but never had I got a chance to make it there before. The moment had come, and I was moving in time to meet this beautiful land ahead. The fellow traveller had told me that this was a place that will remind one of where you have not yet been.

The explorer mind, yes the one that's always there in my life, had woken me up to realise this dream.

I climbed down the mountain filled with curves and headed silently under the shadows of the darkness. I thought for a while that my decision of travelling on a bike was indeed priceless. A drive would not have done the same to me.

I thanked my stars before I made the stop from where the descent to the beach began. Steep winding slopes of steps, with a couple of rocks to avoid in-between, it was right in front of my eyes—the universe had switched on its entertainment channel.

Peace spoke the first of what Gokarna would be.

(As the daylight approached and brightened the light brown sands, souls carrying their thoughts away from the reality were staring straight in to the eyes of the sun. They kept their eyes shut while allowing the sounds coming from the crashing waves gently calm their mind.)

I got myself a place to rest my bones. After finishing a sound breakfast that would hold on until supper, I took a hike to the cliffs that hung closely by the sea front.

I sat there for hours before I would meet any other soul.

The view was magnificent; the palm tree hanging alone at the edge of the cliff spoke a silent story of itself.

I reckon it must have depended on the heart of the person looking at it; everyone saw a different story in it.

When I looked at that palm tree, I could see a sad soul hanging dangerously at the edge of a cliff, unknown of its fate.

But as I gazed through it a moment longer, I saw a different story in it.

I saw in him a brave new soul standing alone at the edge of a dangerous world and changing the view for everyone—just by being where he was.

By it standing at that place where he stood, the beauty of that frame was magnified by the lonely tree.

I laughed at this newfound wisdom and slowly made my way back to the shack where I was put. This time the stars were shining upon me, guiding my way back from a tricky mountain filled with certain death ahead.

I managed to reach the beach. The artificial lights had replaced the natural one. There were folks still playing in the waters, and some of them were lazing on the sand. I made my way straight to my room and changed for the evening in a nice pair of shorts. The sand was still reflecting the warmth they had received from the sun and the air around was warm and inviting.

Night quickly settled in . . .

I finished my supper and went for a round of long walk in the beach that stretched kilometres ahead. The waves fizzled out into small soapy foams while they tried to break the shoreline; the moon happily shared her light to display the funny ambition of the waves. It appeared as if they were conspiring something fun.

I climbed on top of a rock and, gazing at the stars, sat thinking—nothing. I remained in my very own universe.

Early morning, I was woken up by a cold chill. I found myself lying on the beach with sand almost everywhere in my body. I had slept in the open, gazing at the stars. I could not recollect when my eyes gave up on me—I was at peace.

The next day went by exploring other areas of Gokarna. Taking endless boat rides, I went on wild exploration again. Riding high from the foods consumed at the thatched kitchen covering almost every corner of the beach, there was no stopping me. I was happy discovering places that made my heart race with its own rhythm.

I grabbed couple of bottles of release and made my spot at the beach while the evening settled in. I managed to collect a bunch of dead woods and made some arrangements to entertain myself that night.

As the night grew darker, the light from the burning fire lit my world around. I could see an instant reaction to this current flow of event.

A couple of travellers quickly gathered around to warm up their souls with stories from far across the borders. We shared happiness with faces that had never been seen before. The universe had only one topic that night—peace and love.

After a wonderful stay, I returned to Bangalore.

But that soulful trip of mine suddenly rested into an event that would make my life ahead—what it was about to be.

I met with an accident on my return from Gokarna. The next I realised; I was in a hospital; no broken bones but suffered multiple internal injuries.

The doctors strictly advised me a month's rest. I was happy, but Mr Naren had a lot to take care ahead. He had to cancel the shows which had already been scheduled. Losses beyond Mr Naren's interpretation were hovering in front of his eyes, and he did not know what to do.

Behind the mask of a genie, a friend and a well-wisher, he was a shrewd businessman.

He would recover his losses in time.

A month-long recuperating period had me missing my two best friends (guitar and travel).

Mr Naren frequently paid his visits to check if I was all okay and required anything.

Udhav and Nisha also visited often.

Sanjeev had visited me then. It was a pleasant surprise.

(He had seen some reports on my accident and had somehow got my contact number and came to meet me.

We spoke about our good old days, and he mentioned that he missed those days even more.)

Sanjeev for a moment turned a bit emotional when he mentioned that lucky I was to have followed my dreams; as for him, he had to do what he had been told by the crowd.

I didn't know what to tell him then. He thought I was happy; I was happy no doubt; I had always been happy. But there were things that I never understood, and I was chasing it ever since I've had known myself.

(I tried explaining to Sanjeev that happiness was in one's mind, and if you were enjoying every bit of information that a picture could provide; one could see, there were many more things that could make one smile—and it did not depend just on the people or the places.)

He did not understand what I spoke. He said it was easier for me to say as I had managed to reach my dream.

He added, 'Try failing your dream, and you will know who you are instantly.'

After a moment of silence, he then went on to give me an update on Rachel.

(It seems she was doing excellent and had opted to stay back in London and make her living and pursue her career interest.)

Rachel! I thought about her for a while. *I smiled as the thoughts of her seeped my mind.*

Sanjeev smiled at me and jokingly asked if I remembered her. He knew I did—I remained silent.

First show after my accident, and I was happy to be back with my best friend. She tore the crowd apart, and they all went home 'high on music'. I was back with my groove . . .

For a week or so, the happiness of doing what I always have been doing covered the reality away from me. I did not realise I was doing shows almost long-stretched hours in a day. The spotlight that was shining on me, and it had me 'free and high'.

It was only couple of days later the thoughts started to flood my mind.

There was something strange around? My mind was pressing me again, and I was staring at hundreds of answers.

Beam there it came, I was doing shows morning to evening, day and night—exhausted!

When the reality got the better of me, I walked up to Mr Naren to check on it.

He argued that we had too many losses while I was away, and in order to cover it, we had to get going else I would go bankrupt, and the creditors would line up at my house and suck me poor.

He said that litigations would virtually build its prison around me.

When I inquired to him about the money we made from our previous commitments; he shared with me a thick ledger which made no sense to me.

He pointed towards the end where it showed the amount left with us. Not very much was left in it.

He then pointed to the other section where the amount looked magically bigger and mentioned that it was the credit amount we had to clear.

What next, the battle with Guitar began; from that day, somehow she got very annoyed with me.

It refused to be the same. It was a steady decline that was written for me. Though the contract had only couple of months left before it got nullified, my heart was already in a struggle to reach there soon.

Guitar started to speak less about me and started to scream more of how she felt. I would think something, and it would say the exact opposite. The crowd started to relate less with my music, and I needed theatrics to continue with my dream and to find whatever was there to be found.

At some point of time, our hatred got out of line, and I was featured smashing a guitar in one of the newsprint.

It went on to be in the history for sometimes. I hear that they still talk about it.

I must have been insane. Guitar was my best friend and moreover the one I had smashed was priceless. It was a gift from Sir Major, which he had bought for me after he had come to accept my reality.

'What has happened to me?'

(Earlier I used to create energy with my guitar, now I was found doing stunts on the stage.)

I was doing stunts just to keep myself on stage. At first, the crowd fell for my new avatar, and then later, they realised it was a repeat. They slowly turned bored with my dramas.

Mr Naren realised the change in energy and was desperate to get it going. He wanted to extract whatever he could until the last day of the contract.

He did all he could to get the most before his windfall got over and had my schedule running packed; With this, new schedules around his hands were got shorter every single day, and he needed some help pronto, and he got one.

He hired an assistant for himself; her name was Medha Menon, and she was to be my new genie. All I had to do was ask her.

But she had to be told well in advance if only you wanted your order to arrive in time.

She drove me insane when I was already running high on it.

(Initially I had a discussion with Mr Naren on the sudden change of arrangements but had no go with his arguments which was well armed with his well-chosen words. I had to agree to what he had to disagree.)

However, she had her own way of making use of humour as her defence. *Let's just say she survived the next couple of months working with me.*

As time flew by a little, I got to know from Medha that she was also from the same college that I attended. Oh, the next big surprise, she was from the same batch as mine and had been an acquaintance of Dechen and had visited the United Nation on several occasions.

I was surprised and with an apologetic face let her know that I had never seen her face before.

Apparently, she was Dechen's classmate and used to tag along with her at times whenever she visited us.

I wore a blank face while she had me filled with her memories from the cafeteria.

What can I say, sometimes memories fail you?

The last few months—left with the contract with Mr Naren and all hell broke loose.

Mr Naren's ambition had reached its limits, and my relationship was already in a bad shape with Guitar. As you know by now, she was making me do things I had never imagined.

Travel had disappeared for a while as most of the last-moment commitments were within the city. There had been a sudden change in the music culture and more tolerable audiences were gathering for the concerts.

This was the time of gold rush for the musicians as quoted by Mr Naren.

And as for me, I was in no mood to collect any of it.

I was on stage only to pass on the messages; instead, I was being asked to collect charity.

I was running, scared with the fear of losing what I did not even have before; I went on marching with my heart left somewhere else. They were terrible dark days!

Medha was mostly the victim of my misplaced anger. *Poor soul, I hope she has forgiven me.*

Mr Naren too was not spared from it, but my anger towards him was for real. Somewhere deep down, I knew he was aware of how I felt for him and yet he felt nothing to stop whatever he was doing to me. I was there helpless, tied in the web as desired by the mass.

He had an option to let the time roll by slowly, but instead, he chose to fast forward the moments for me.

Did I hate him?

Of course, you bet.

(No man living in this world should treat anyone like he had done to me. He took me to a fairy land and showed me around. Then he traded me with the devil and left home rich. I thought he was there to show me better days and let me discover life as I had to understand. Instead . . .)

Instead, he wanted to get the clock speeding around me.

Where has it left me today with all those experiences?

Don't worry, there are many more stories in-between before Mr Naren and I shared our final goodbyes.

In those last few days a lot changed . . . Just hang in there.

By now the spirits in me had started to feel the extreme change of flow in the energy within my universe. They went on a wild exploration from where the time had to be suspended and memories were less available in there. Everything healed by itself rather quickly.

My lazy little soul craved the company of the universe that was brightly lit by imaginations.

I forgot everything; while my body was being dragged into selling itself to survive, my soul remained unchanged. But my heart? By then, it was everywhere.

The sudden change in the energy inside had led to a conflict between spirits residing inside me, and my heart not much around to control, I was about to go rebel.

Mr Naren did what he could; it was time for me to do what I had to.

Guitar and I spoke very less to each other those days, and the faces had started to rapidly shrink at my shows. Mr Naren was not bothered at all. The sponsors had already paid him his booking amount and nothing could go wrong for him.

And if anything at all, it would have been the sponsors loss and not his. He was a smart businessman.

(I felt betrayed; I trusted him as my friend and a brother, and when I look back, all he has done is used my talent to make some money for him. He cared less to what happened to me. The genie he was to me was just to ensure he had me in his spell. There was no care to whatever he did.)

I then looked at Medha.

Any sweet word from her would pierce me like a sharp needle. I would draw up a quick comparison with how exactly Mr Naren used to be and then got reminded of the image of how he turned out to be—filled with loathe and bitterness.

She might have thought I must have gone crazy.

Most of the times, my heart would be around to control the spirit in me whenever it differed. But then again, whenever it went missing, she would feel the pinch.

It was a promotional show for a cell phone company who was trying to expand their customer base, and I was to perform as the guest artist and was to leave the venue as soon as possible.

That night the venue was running a little packed, and the crowd had in quite a number to see me perform. I only had one song to share; yet there were people flocking all over the place and filling it up to grab a glimpse.

(Mr Naren hoped that the goodwill event for the service provider would secure the upcoming shows for him.)

One must be taking a long walk with his thoughts every day, only then one could think like Mr Naren.

He was already building future plans while I was still staring at my present and wondered, what had happened to it?

I was an hour late reaching the venue that evening, and by then, the crowd had grown a little annoyed with the delayed entry.

I could hear comments being thrown at me as I made my way to the makeshift stage at the mall.

I started off with my performance without any care to the flowing abuses of the mass, coming from all directions.

I was busy trying to reconcile with the Guitar.

The Guitar chose not to forgive me then.

Everyone thought success was riding me high . . . . Media got their scoop that night, and it was seen splashed all over in the morning gossip column.

(I never cared to explain to the crowd why I was late that day. They would have never understood. But let the truth be shared to those reading this book: Medha had got my schedule all jumbled up that day, and in confusion, we ended up reaching a bit late to the venue.)

What else am I forgetting about that evening? . . . Oh! I now remember, that evening I met Nadja . . .

. . . Again!

She happened to be in the same mall where I was to perform. She came by to say 'hello' post my performance.

'What was she doing there in the mall? Okay, let's forget the mall. What was she doing in Bangalore? No, not just Bangalore, what was she doing in India?'

Thought she had said her goodbyes long ago . . .

Anyway, I was glad to see a known face again.

After old faces disappearing from my life, life had taught me to value pictures from the memories even more and seeing Nadja back in town, it was a refreshing sight.

(I learnt her return to Bangalore was on a business. Oh, I forgot, after her return to Germany, she had managed to secure a job in a reputed media firm, and in time, she had climbed up the ladder and was now presented with the opportunity to spearhead a critical project in their Bangalore office. She informed she would be in Bangalore for a long time.)

We shared our contact numbers and left with a promise to catch up again.

After a week, Nadja called up to check my calendar. We planned to catch up soon.

She was seated with a mug of beer at the corner of the garden restaurant where we were to meet.

(The restaurant had a small water fountain giving the feel of a rushing stream as if born out of a heavenly monsoon, and the garden extended itself indoor—to an open lounge. I felt at peace instantly.)

There she was—fair, white porcelain-skinned, blonde hair held back tightly, only a few loose strands of it were allowed to fall on her face. Her eyes were marine blue, and it was staring right back into mine—as if it was always questioning something. And at that very moment, she wore a smile one could never ignore.

We sat hours with our share of drinks and were filling each other with our stories that had been so far—mostly it was hers. For some reason, she already knew an awful lot about me. I thought it must have been the media that would have fed her with enough update on me.

Those gossips can really sell millions.

I sensed a dramatic change in her, and she was extraordinarily nice to me. She was keen on knowing every bit of the story of my life; I wondered why?

She later confessed to have voluntarily taken up the job assignment in Bangalore as she strongly felt that her education from India would help her add 'value' to the project she was to lead. I felt a lot had changed in her.

Though I knew she was someone who was never afraid to venture the 'unknown', seeing herself in the new avatar, I must admit, I was impressed.

It reminded me of the palm tree, how it had sacrificed everything to be wherever it had to be and add a different dimension to the entire picture . . . Amazing!

Quickly our conversation touched its direction towards much serious note in her life.

She was upset over the situation with her landlord.

She had rented an apartment with a year's lease, but the owner decided not to let her keep the house after she had shifted in and had asked her to vacate the apartment at the earliest.

She was running worried and did not know why the landlord was doing what he had been doing, and it made her wonder why had he had turned so rude—so sudden. She concluded that complaining to the authorities was neither an option—it always fell into deaf ears and a waste of time and loss of money.

She then asked if I knew any place that was up for rent. I wasn't aware of any, and as I was stressing myself hard to remember if I had come across any house up for a rent . . .

. . . She went on to inquire about my place. I gave her a brief description of it.

She further inquired if anyone lived in the other room. I told her I used it for store, and at times, it doubled as guest room.

She was lost in her thoughts for a while and then she asked if she could stay at my place. She was pretty direct with her request.

I thought for a while . . .

She then added, only if I was comfortable with it.

I argued with my thoughts, 'She might have been desperate to get a place to stay.'

It was a long pause before I agreed to share my apartment with her. She moved in the next day.

After she was done neatly packing her belongings inside the cupboard, she asked me if I could get her a coffee. I went ahead and got one ready for her.

She went curious as to why I did not make one for myself.

I told her I was not in a mood at the moment.

She chuckled, as if to say, *'Too bad for you.'*

Whatever, she was a pretty straight forward person, and I took no offence to what she had to say. Only in time, I would get to know what was really in her mind.

You see time brings in comfort, and once you start sharing your space with someone, the comfort seems to enter much faster than one might have imagined.

It was only when Nadja and I started to share the apartment, I realised she had been suffering from a terrible anger disorder and had been having her regular anger therapies—ever since her childhood.

She had been in therapy sessions even while she was in college, and it was the only reason how she could keep her anger anchored then.

A critical observation I made on Nadja was that her uncontrollable anger only went up to a verbal massacre which could slice anyone on its way—yet, somehow in her expression, she made it clear that she did not want to hurt anyone.

When I look back, I realise she had never thrown her anger fits to anyone in India before. She had always chosen to stay away from anything that had her mood altered. It was only me who had got the little taste of it, and with her staying at my place, it became a regular affair.

I had been made aware by her for the anger behind our initial days . . . But the one I got to see during her stay at my apartment, God only knows where she got energy to cook such a storm.

Anyway, it took me no time to get used to her mood swings. I went a mute crusade whenever she had her relapses, and she got nothing from me to throw back at.

With all of her drama, her presence at my house somehow made me feel safe. Safe that someone familiar and long lost from a time was somewhere close by me. There were no new faces to pull me apart.

With days moving by quickly, time got Nadja and me closer. We became friends, the good ones, of course.

With the latest shades that had been painting pictures around, she would be home, and just to see her present in the frame brought me an unknown peace.

She would ask a lot of questions, and she would try to justify my thoughts.

She was a mind stealer. She could get inside my head, read it, manipulate it, feed stories to it, yet somehow she did it just to get me through those days.

There we were enjoying the madness together and thanking each other for just being present in each other's life. (At least that is what I think.)

As the dramas were unfolding, one fine day, I got a call from my dad, and he wanted to know the story at my end.

It seems he had read some news that had pictures from my previous melodrama.

(The one that had me featured smashing my guitar. Lucky for me, he did not recognise the guitar in the picture.)

I told him that it was a marketing gimmick, and it was a part of our planned strategy to boost my image.

He bought it.

Well, I could not understand him clearly, but he said something which sounded like okay and then handed over the phone to my mom.

Mom—she talked about how everyone spoke to her in the town, and how well-known she was—as my mom, in the crowd around.

I inquired if she liked the attention, and she said she did. It made her feel special.

She never asked if I ever liked the attention; she assumed I was happily living my dream.

But reality spoke different; I was there, stuck in a tug of war between what I loved and what needed to be done.

6

The last few months had dragged itself into a 'Rip Van Winkle' year. The time had stretched itself into a never-ending nightmare, and I wanted to wake up—badly.

On hindsight, I wouldn't call it a nightmare; it was more of a dream that needed a different start.

The days overextended itself, and the night took its own sweet time to arrive. And as soon as the night said hello, the day came by rather quick to greet again and dragged me back to the place I hated the most. Sometimes even nights pulled me there . . .

Every time I returned home after a brutal day with 'hate and betrayal', I was welcomed by Nadja. Her presence had helped me pick up the pieces of the torn paintings and piece it together.

(She helped me complete the pictures ahead. She never gave up her 'hope' on me.)

Hope—isn't it what makes this world go crazy? Just a tiny little four-letter word and you know what it does?

It does what no other word existing in this universe can do. It puts an empty canvas in front of you—drags you to fit in and then leaves you hanging in the frame . . . Smile!

So what I had to be introduced to hope the way I had to be?

I always knew what it was . . . But what it meant? Well, one has to wait for what the lessons can leave you with.

(Something you don't know about hope. It is not just one big picture that you finally end up drawing. Hope is about those tiny pictures that make that final portrait.

'Yes, now you understand.'

Hope makes you paint those tiny little paintings which you have been ignoring for a long time and slowly, but steadily, it starts to shape into a bigger picture you might have imagined to be your masterpiece.)

Anyway, as hope helped me move along this time, I was happy Nadja and I had grown to be good friends.

While I was spending more and more time closing tight schedules ahead—*(honestly most of my efforts were being diverted in trying to avoid Mr Naren and the stage, and the guitar equally trying to avoid me)*—I was always happy to be home at the end of the day.

As you read earlier, guitar had suddenly turned into this evil friend of mine . . . She always left me running behind and refused to listen to me.

The stage had become my circus and the fans and my followers were struggling to identify with the new message I brought along.

I had become a joker, the one which Mr Naren had helped create.

'Blame it on Mr Naren,' *I told myself. I told myself to blame it on him for all the wrong he had done to me.*

Getting rid of guilt can be a long painful journey, especially the guilt of losing a friend—and in this case, it was my best friend—Guitar.

I survived this long journey in space and time by reminding myself of my real purpose for being here. (Share the messages of the universe with everyone—through my music.)

Adit surprised me with his Bangalore visit, just before I parted my ways with Mr Naren.

He was equally surprised to see Nadja in my apartment. It must have been my honest omission not informing him on her stay. Anyway, he was glad to see Nadja, and there was a bit of emotions running high in the living room that day.

Soon they were updating each other with their stories from the time—they had lost contact.

I was in the kitchen, preparing coffee for everyone; after sometime, Adit walked in and gave me a dry smile. He had a smile that would not wipe away.

I moved my eyebrows in upward direction, suggesting him to spill it out.

As the story goes, Adit was getting married soon . . .

Getting married? Thought he was always running away from commitment?

Well! What can we say to the ways of the universe . . . I inquired about the wedding date? Stupid of me then, I forgot to ask him about the bride (Who was she? What did she do? Where did she come from? Blah . . . blah . . . blah . . .)

I think the question Adit was eagerly waiting to be asked was—'Who was the lucky girl?'

He made the same face again, and he kept staring at me. There was a mute moment between us.

Somehow, the question he had been eagerly waiting to come out from my mouth—'Who was the lucky lady?'—finally found its words.

He smiled and replied. Reena, his childhood friend! Though we had not met, I recollect Adit mention her name before.

Apparently, a lot had happened in the last six months since we had last spoken to each other. Who knew, in time, Adit was to marry Reena. Although he had mentioned about her before, but I never thought she would end up as his life partner.

After Adit had returned to Delhi, he had ventured into a small construction business and as destiny happened to be, Adit met Reena.

Reena had returned from Canada after finishing her architectural course and happened to have applied for a position of an architect in his firm. Both were unaware of their current reality, and when time brought them together, the stupid cupid had bigger plan for both . . . They were to find togetherness with each other for the rest of their life.

I invited Nisha and Udhav over to my place to join us for a small gathering to celebrate Adit's happiness.

Nadja had gone out to get the spirits in hers uplifted.

After everyone was done doing what they had to do and had joined us in our celebration, we sat on the balcony, glasses filled optimistically, gazing at the sky. The sky wore dark angry face that night. It was about to rain, and Nadja had still not returned.

It wasn't until nine, and the rain was still on its pouring spree, she finally arrived. She greeted everyone and went straight to her room. She bought an excuse to get herself changed. I knew she looked a little buzzed at that moment.

I allowed that moment to pass by; she walked her way to her room. 'Let it be,' I told to myself.

There was madness screaming so loud, neighbours had to drop by twice requesting to keep it decent.

Nadja kept on shuttling between her room and the living area and cared none to join us in our celebration.

By then the rain had cleaned the air. Even the mosquitoes flying around could be seen, a good fifty yards ahead. Darn, it rained as if it was some kind of charity event that was organised by our politicians. Yes, the ones that happen just before the time when papers are in our hand and a box in front to drop by. It rained as if someone had promised a monsoon during draught season and then without any trace, it stopped.

The rain brought a different mood along with it . . .

Adit and his never-ending imagination made us take our wheels to a small get-away place from the city.

On our way ahead, we were about to hit a detour, which I was not prepared for . . . I was yet to be made aware of . . .

The road went narrowing down to smaller gullies, and as we moved ahead, we reached the turn from where the journey to our escape was towards left.

However, Nadja insisted we take right. The road to it looked less maintained . . .

I told her the way to our destination was left. She said she knew about it, but she wanted to explore the other place that she had read about, somewhere. It was a place seldom visited by any.

She argued the mountains which the regulars enjoyed frequently were known to many, but this one was an unchartered land, and it promised an adventure that would introduce us to a brand-new picture which would only remain forever—engraved in our memories.

I gave a good look to myself at the rear-view mirror and examined my thoughts carefully. I was not prepared for this sudden change in plan and yet something in me said it was something what had to be done.

'Just let the moments decide.'

The wheels turned right, and the girls went on a howling spree.

The night was half lit by the healing moon. The road revealed itself under the bright neons of the car. The mountain foxes from far across, time and again howled towards the direction we were travelling. *They must have thought it was their lovers' call when they heard the girls scream.*

We reached a foothill from where the car had to be given away. The only tool available to take you to the top would be your very own two legs. The prize for reaching the top after a steep rocky uphill climb was a view only time could have revealed.

Adit, Udhav, and Nisha sat halfway through to rest their heartbeat. After they had their rhythm in-sync they again slowly marched uphill. I looked at them from a little above. Nadja was standing next to me.

Nadja placed a bet to race to the mountain top. *The bet was for the loser to confess whatever the winner asks.*

I knew I would win the race, and I had nothing to hide; I smiled and agreed to her whimsy.

And as the stories are to be told in time, drums rolled, and the gang of monkeys hanging precariously on the treetops greeted me with their loud cheer when I reached the finish line. It took a while before the blur in my eyes caused due to extreme determination of winning the race finally settled down. Well, as the view in front of me cleared, I saw Nadja smiling at me . . . waiting.

Yes, yours truly lost.

I remember telling myself at that grand moment, 'Shame it was to have lost to Nadja. Let's see what I have got to confess.'

Nadja wore the same face she had for Jacob, when I had first seen her. I believe she acquired that look mostly to patronise someone and yet it somehow appeared to be innocent and harmless.

I knew what she meant.

Disgrace! And I felt like one. I had lost to Nadja.

(Whatever happened to all those marine trainings we had to undergo during our school days? We were made to run 100 steps—squatting down, trudging through the gushing streams made from sprinkling rain and still . . . Ah, forget about it . . . I lost.)

Nadja had another trick neatly tucked up under her imagination. She said she did not want me to confess anything at that moment. She wanted to hold on with her question until the moment was right. I the gentleman made no fuss on it.

It was an hour-long wait before others would finally catch up with us.

Settled that she would ask the question whenever she wanted to ask, we sat there quietly, letting our thoughts observe the beauty of clouds floating beneath those mountains.

Moments passed away, drawing images on those dark grey clouds hanging below before we picked up our conversation again.

It had been sometime that Nadja had remained a constant face in my life, and our friendship had grown into a more tolerable one. I guess we both knew that our hearts judged each other, no more.

She told me she wanted to paint her room and was not sure if I would allow her to do so. I told her that it was her house too; she could change anything that she wanted in it.

The one and only condition . . .

Apart from changing the 'kirpan' and the 'khukuri' from where it was, I guess I was okay to see a new frame by then. I made it clear to her, and she agreed.

Soon, we found ourselves talking about my experiences and the topics somehow stretched and I was found talking at length about the three of us—(Travel, Guitar, and myself.)

It was only after Nadja interrupted me with her uncontrollable laughter, I realised my thoughts had caught the better of my mouth.

Somehow my conversation had reached its journey and had revealed the secret adventures of mine. *You know, the one that happens on stage. Yes, you got it right, the stunts I carry out during days whenever there is fight with the guitar.*

She must have laughed for a whole minute or so while her laughter turned me mute. Slowly recovering herself and wiping tears away from her eyes, she remained within her own universe for a while.

There was a moment of deafness in the air, but periodically, it could be heard talking mind games.

It started off with a whisper which gradually gained its volume when she went on to narrate the story, the one she had never shared before . . .

I listened to her without giving away anything that was running on my mind . . .

She continued . . .

Remember, me telling before how I never listened to Nadja and that it helped me get through those early years? It wasn't until that moment when she asked me a question. *'Kabir, what do you think of love?'*

I answered her it would depend on what the definition of love is for an individual.

She quoted, 'Love is just an insecurity which everyone wants to share.'

That was the time when I really listened to her; never before had I paid her any real good attention.

She asked me for the definition I shared on love; and just when I was about to echo my thoughts, the conversation was quickly hijacked by Adit, who had made it to the summit and had been going hysterical. He was screaming to the open and thanking the unknown for the opportunity given to experience nature's live show.

The rest of the troupe joined a little later, and we left our conversation to where it had reached at that point in time.

*About spending another hour and a*fter much painful trek downhill, we finally arrived to the spot where we had parked the car. Nadja insisted that she would drive. I gave her the keys.

Somehow she knew I would not refuse even though it was written all over my bulletin board—car and guitar were something that I never shared with anyone.

We whooshed back to the city. The roads had just started to grow much friendly after a long off-road tour, and Nadja had a face one could not forget. (It read, the speed was her best friend, and she was racing to meet her again.)

I reminded her to keep it under 100, and the moment I completed my sentence, the speedometer had the reading of 120. She looked at me and passed a snide comment. She told me I should get my heart replaced; the one that I had was a bit too weakened by fear, she added.

Completing her sentence, she raised the accelerator, and the needle in the speedometer jumped past 160. No one complained; it must have been the closed windows of the car that somehow prevented the folks behind from realising the actual speed of our travel.

And I was there, staring straight into it—as the needle slowly pushed its way forward. It wasn't a pleasant feeling to be seated right next to her.

I wouldn't say it was fear, but the sudden realisation of how different both our universe was made me constantly remind her to slow down the vehicle. More my words fell to her ears, the heavier her foot got on to the gas paddle.

Before the unwarranted race reached us to our destination, I lost two days of my life. I was lying in the hospital, unconscious.

Luck dragged me back into my reality and the advancement in science gave me back my life.

The rest of the folks had managed to escape with minor scratches and bruises. Nadja had been suffering mild concussions, and for me, I had banged my head so hard on the safety bag, it felt like a brick wall upon impact. With no broken bones, I thanked the Lord for saving me.

However, it took the lights off from me for two whole days.

While I was on my unplanned hibernation, Mr Naren yet again, had been facing a lot of heat from the promoters and the investors. They had already diverted their fund for the events and had thought of getting a large return on it.

Mr Naren had his own ambitions of making the most before the contract with me got over. This time he had felt the change in energy around and was running scared I might not renew the contract. *What can one do for a diseased mind?*

After skipping two days of my life, I was allowed back to my apartment. Mr Naren came by later to pay his visit.

He told me that there was news for me: one, of course, was a good one, and the other was rather not-so-good one. He asked me which one I would prefer to listen first.

I went with the good one first. He went on to update me that even though there had been some issues and concerns with the investors, the new person in me had also brought a new set of followers, a complete different fan following, and they were waiting for me to share the messages with them.

I asked him to continue sharing the bad one.

He said that the days lost due to the unforeseen event had cost us real big and damages were running into amount beyond imagination and the investors wanted a payback. I forgot to check for the clauses that was cleverly inserted by them and had got me sign their will to share my messages across.

Who knew about that day?

(Darn those vultures. I was spreading messages about humanity, and they were already waiting for me to drop dead and feast upon.)

I told Mr Naren to give them whatever it takes to get me back myself—my freedom.

Mr Naren suggested he too had some pending cheques which needed to be cleared at the earliest for him. It was for the services he had rendered upon me for being my genie.

I wasn't bothered much and told him to share me the final report on what was what after settling my dues.

Nadja spoke nothing about the accident to me; instead, later when she found me alone, she came to me and asked how I was feeling.

'Awesome!' went my prompt reply—she smiled at me and then she asked . . . 'Kabir, I think it is time I get to know your definition on love.'

I was surprised with her casual attitude. But then, I went ahead sharing what I thought about it . . .

I never understood what this whole world spoke on love. It was a bit too confusing for me to understand what others understood.

I told her I guess it was my whole different understanding of this universe that made me who I was. She waited without any change of expression on her and allowed me to share the definition on it . . .

'Love for me is unknown, unknown how far it stretches. So the way I see love is . . . ,' I went on, 'Love is just an ordinary word that describes extraordinary moments.'

I love being in the world that I am, no matter how it maybe, the only time sadness bestows me is when I realise that I am no longer me.

'Like the ones on the stage?' Nadja inquired.

'That's correct,' I responded to her.

'What makes you feel, that you are not you?'

I don't know why I was sharing what I was sharing with her, but I went on explaining how I loved Guitar, and the love we both shared for one another was beyond any explanation and that our love was unknown—it was boundless—infinite and never ending. We could stay mad with each other, but we knew deep down we could never stay apart—for long.

Nadja remained silent for a while, then she repeated— Love is unknown. Her eyes had turned red; she hurriedly made way to her room and locked herself in.

Adit had been observing this all the while from a distance. He came to check if I had said something about the accident to her. I assured him that I had not. I was as surprised as he was to see her reaction then.

The night continued as it had been moments earlier, *but there was a silence that had been planted in my head that night. It was only starting to slowly grow.*

The day to freedom was just a walk away, and with Adit back in the picture, life had turned itself to a circus again.

Guitar and I had been slowly working with our differences, and it was me working harder this time to be who I used to be.

But the curious mind kept telling me that I have something more to learn and explore.

At that very moment I reminded myself not to listen to the curious mind any more. Everything was getting better. The time had moved its needle, and it was ticking for a better tomorrow . . . I consoled myself . . . *Tick-tock.*

It was time for Adit to part from us again. Nadja and I promised him our presence on his big day.

The moment arrived when I was finally free from the majority's prison. I was free from the contractual ties that my soul had been pledged against. My heart knew no bounds and was filled with happiness. I went to share my happiness with Guitar, and she spoke to me with all the joy she had in her. It gave birth to a fresh new message; it was a song not heard before.

I went ahead and shared the newfound message on the public portal. Before I could realise, there were people talking about my newfound music again. This time the audience had seen themselves in a revolution of time, and the crowd wore faces that all looked the same. No race, no caste, no creed—it was a face of humanity. Hundreds of thousands who viewed the recordings posted their gratitude for sharing the message across. The asked me to share more of it.

Guitar, she reminded me to go slow this time.

One at a time, one at a time—she whispered through my ears.

Mr Naren paid his visit to my apartment after hearing my newfound viral success. He wanted me to reconsider his services if I ever wanted to get back to where he thought I should be. I told him with all my humility that I would let him know whenever I decided what I would be deciding.

I told him that I was taking it slow . . .

———◦◦═◦◦———

Days moved ahead inching itself. I discovered a whole new universe with music this time. There was no pressure of being where I had to be. I spent my time with guitar hours at a stretch, writing new messages— messages that could make a soul come alive.

Travel never complained. Not that I had forgotten her—she was my best friend too, but she was someone who did not need my assurance every time. We knew we missed each other.

Days had gone unrevealing the newfound messages. Nadja had been her usual self—*timely sharing her temper lapses, still no harm reported to any.*

There's nothing I could have done to help her.

Never knew what made her so angry.

(It was only one fine day when I watched a movie on their fuhrer, it was then when I watched his temper fly; I mean literally that man had so much sore in his mouth that when he spoke his thoughts, saliva went rocketing into the nose of a general standing close to him. I could clearly see the expressions on that gentleman's face. The camera had got it all . . .

A disgusted fairly old man trying to find a gas mask to protect himself from the stinging chemical droplets, yet he had no choice but to remain calm and collected in front the mad man . . . as he kept his wish lists in front of them . . .

Did I realise why Nadja's anger went uncontrollable at times?

Well, everybody loves attention, and somehow they get whatever they wished for—through madness at times.

It was around seven in the evening and the doorbell rang, and as I went to answer the door and receive, whoever it was, at that time . . .

Sir Major and Mom were standing, smiling—surprise!

I don't know what got into Sir Major, but that day he hugged me tight.

I walked them inside, and they saw Nadja seated on the sofa, reading magazine.

Sir Major gave a sharp look at me and moved his gaze towards Mom.

His inquired Mom if she had any prior knowledge about the lady's presence in my apartment.

Mom wore a blank face and went curious too.

Before I could say something, Nadja approached my parents and went introducing herself.

While she kept the conversation flowing with my parents, she had gone an extra mile to add a 'namaste' to both of them, before she got herself introduced.

Mom, Pariniti, was floored by this sudden cultural surprise coming from a gori.

She went on to add, back in their own home town, where people were considered to be culturally polite and a namaste was a must for every greeting to elders, it had seen a sharp extinction. Here she was receiving the highest degree of respect that she considered for herself—from a Westerner.

It instantly took Nadja to be framed in one of the picture that my mom keeps carrying around her heart. *Not many in it, but Nadja managed to get there somehow.*

The night went by rather quickly, and Mom and Dad retired into my room. I went hanging my legs neatly stretched in lounge at the living room. The lounge was running a bit shorter for me. I was thinking about my parents' sudden visit to Bangalore. I knew it had been some time I had not seen them, but they always kept me updated with their travel plans . . . whenever it was to happen. This time it was uncharacteristic of Sir Major—a surprise visit. Something must be there, I thought . . .

The next day was welcomed by a surprise breakfast that was prepared by my mom and Nadja. It would be this day that Sir Major settled that gori girls too were cultured.

If only they had seen the anger in her, I am sure they would have got their return tickets sooner than they would have thought.

Sir Major was curious to know more of my stories and was always running behind me with his questions.

This had started to grow on me and had begun pressing the air around . . . What more, Mom joined Dad in his struggle . . .

It was time for me to disappear in my own little universe.

'How . . . ?'

I got three movie tickets to a new release. *It was the first day, first show,* and I shelled a fortune to get the tickets from behind the counters.

Handing over the tickets to their newfound best friend, I asked Nadja to take them to the movie; she agreed instantly . . .

Surprised a little myself to see Nadja agree instantly, I could see the smile on my parents' face, and it was the one I had never seen before.

It was a good three to four hours of relief for me—good riddance!

(The media had fed my parents' mind with loads of gossip which they had started to believe to be true. And it seems their surprise visit was a way to check upon the reality for me. *I can never teach a mind that has already taught itself not to learn.*)

It was a moment of release—the universe in me had settled down and had been hungry for some time to learn more on what could be the messages that had in time to reveal. *Lessons that I still had to earn to learn were brewing along, I was oblivious then.*

It was around nine, and I was at the balcony, watching stars and Mom and Dad were watching television. Nadja stepped into the balcony and inquired how I was doing.

I replied life was as it was—good.

She went on a mute campaign for a while before she came back with her questions again. She asked me if there was something wrong with me. She wanted to know why I did not take my parents to the movie and had asked her instead.

I looked at her. She knew nothing what she was talking about, but she wanted to know if it was anything at all.

I wanted to share with her the lessons, the messages, and what it spoke to me about the entire reality.

Ever since my existence, I had my own understanding of relations between everything that surrounded me and yet I could not explain it to anyone.

The only way I could try and explain reality came in the form of my messages—through my Guitar and my songs. Only few could understand the dreams it stole from the one who played those messages, yet the majority understood very little.

My mouth gave a dry run, but the words were left unspoken. However, time had funny lessons to speak for itself.

Nadja's proximity with my parents had transformed to be the bridge for them to know me better. They spoke about the big question mark which I had always been— they laughed—whenever Sir Major would talk about my childhood memories.

Mom went a bit over the board to keep the laughter going . . .

She revealed one of my embarrassing childhood moment, Sir Major was particularly not amused with the joke; he was a gentleman who would not laugh at such a poorly played joke in front of a lady.

They would discuss my habits and complained how oblivious I remained from the reality . . .

I quietly observed their thesis on me and whispered to myself, 'Just hold on to your reality. Time will come soon when reality shall have itself revealed.'

Time will come soon, for what exactly?

That was something I was not aware myself.

All I knew was that time never stood still and always brought fresh new pictures along. Good or bad, it did not matter to it. Time brought whatever it had to bring along, and it would be our job to learn and let it be.

Had I shared what I had in my mind then with Nadja, I am pretty sure she would have shared it with Sir Major and with my mom. With Nadja's proximity to my parents, I refrained to explain.

I thought for a while, 'Why did I even try explaining something to her, which I had never tried explaining to anyone else before?'

Once more, time did what it always done. After a week's stay, my parents decided it was time they made their way back home. A week with them around—felt like an eternity, never had I felt the same. It was only then when I realised why I had tried explaining the reality with Nadja.

Nadja had made my parents walk half way through to the world the one I lived in. She had made them walk there and made them look at me from the distance from where they would better understand who I had always been.

I had started to trust her even more and saw her as the bridge that would bring my parents into my universe.

She had made them realise why I had been around with bigger questions running inside me. She made them realise that my struggle had not been so clear to everyone—I was far away from the universe of others, finding my own reality. I guess she had slowly started to understand the messages of my guitar. Though I am not sure if she did indeed, but she had learnt to pick its subtle messages at times.

I was here for a bigger cause and not just to survive.

———

Nadja was wearing a pink kurta, the one my parents had gifted her before they left. She was thrilled to wear the Indian attire and was cursing herself for not having tried the Indian dresses before. She thought it would never complement her Western skin. *She was wrong . . . It looked amazing on her.*

Eureka moment of hers lasted for another month. Nadja was only to be seen in Indian attire—kurtas and pyjamas. At times, she made good use of her fine fashion faculties and wore jeans underneath instead of the pyjamas and wore a thin beige-coloured scarf, which covered her head to protect it from the city air. The air taxed by the cost of human development, she also extended the scarf to cover her face, revealing only her blue eyes.

In those few days, I saw slight changes in Nadja. It appeared as if her anger had suddenly found some other anchor to hold on to.

Not that she had got rid of it completely, but she had become someone who had started to look at life a little different and had begun to feel less pressed around. God knows what message she had been receiving, but I was happy that she was happy.

This was a moment when life suddenly stopped transmitting messages, and I was getting to know the silence better. I was floating in a field of ecstasy. Life had become what it had become, and I welcomed where I stood then.

I thought life's lessons must have been over. I must have been done with the messages, I reassured myself . . .

(The new messages I had shared through the public portal found a new life of its own. It reached an unseen popularity, and the crowd was demanding for a concert.

The crowds went chanting mad, but I was happy being behind the scene and sharing whatever I had to share, and this time I was doing it without pressing the air much around me. Music spoke the universal language, and my fans were quickly erasing their borders.)

I felt I had discovered what the curious mind had always wanted me to find through the messages—the messages that wanted take everyone to a brand-new world, and I was the only one who knew the map to it.

A land where everyone was united by one thought (no judgements) and one care (no fakes). A place where one could be themselves or whoever they could be.

Reach the stars through your dreams and fuel it with the soul that feeds on a never-ending adventure had been the motto of my life.

Life had opened a brand-new door for me to find and share the message without harming myself.

Nadja was in the living room reading what the rest of the city read—'the gossip'.

Nadja suddenly shouted out loud, this one not her usual spells.

She showed me an article with 'gossips' written all over it.

It wrote the new songs that I had shared through the post had managed to break new craze, and the crowd wanted me back, from where they could see me perform once again.

Nadja went on to update me that she had received a call from her old acquaintance who had been following my music closely and wanted to offer me an opportunity to share it live with the top musicians of the world. I was to share the platform as a guest performer in the concert which he was organising.

I had already found a new platform to share my messages; the newfound platform was comfortable, and it allowed me to be who I had to be. I humbly declined the offer.

It wasn't until he spoke to Nadja again and had her feed my mind, I agreed to his terms and conditions.

Nadja told me that I could meet up with travel again. It had been a long time since I had greeted Travel, and I thought it was a good opportunity and thought what harm it could bring.

It was Mumbai, and the crowd were in millions, shouting for the messages to be shared. I heard a loud roar when the gods entered the arena, carrying their weapons that shot raw music through the ears, loud enough to kill your heart, yet gentle enough to let it remain unharmed. Their messages were masked in their performance; it had to be observed carefully. They were speaking of unknowns.

Hour-long preaching, and it was their time to take a break. Quickly I was asked to take my position and make my way to the stage.

I could hear insanity hovering around, and once again people were waiting to greet me.

Once again the blood settled in quickly and filled my heart till it could hold no more, and then the heart squeezed itself rapidly, shooting blood straight towards the veins that was running all over my fingers. I could feel the energy pulsating all over my body; it was time to wake up, music was spilling all over the air.

The crowd welcomed me back with much love and care; they heard my new messages and this time they understood it much better.

The gods themselves joined me later, and shared the stage with me.

I became one with the person that I was always supposed to be—answers completed my soul that night. At least, that is what I thought.

———————⚬⟐⚬———————

Media had got hold of some gossips and had printed an exaggerated story on me. It was the same media firm where Nadja was employed.

Not that it covered the entire story of my entire life, but it had substantial amount of gossips that were supported by facts, built in someone's grand imagination, which led to unwarranted attention from Sir Major.

At first, I thought it might have been Nadja who would have had something to do with the column printed in her magazine. She strongly protested against and mentioned that she would never use our friendship to gain heights in her career. She promised me to find out the real culprit behind printing such a baseless report.

Before my memories got imprinted permanently with the sad episode of my life, I found myself again drifting into my own universe. Travel had given me the opportunity to visit Mumbai, the city of hopes and dreams and it was time to explore.

Mumbai took my breath away. The necklace road proudly stretched miles ahead and lit up the entire city with its magical charm. While the beauty of the city was beyond words to describe, the poorly lit slums reflected a deep scar to it.

It only reflected the reality of what greed can do to humanity—the rich were getting richer, and the have-nots were being threatened with their existence.

The city was moving ahead in time, but the faces disappeared sooner than one could have thought it would generally take.

While Travel took me around the city and got me introduced to new landscapes and other interesting personalities—some well-known figures of the country renowned in their field of art It was here I met Mr Parimal Gautam, whom I fondly referred to as PG.

PG was a jovial old businessman. We met through a common friend, and later, he had approached me to share the messages on behalf of him. He wanted to sign up a contract with me. I told him that I would think about it and let the moment pass.

Storm of thoughts was battling inside me, and it took some time to settle down . . .

I knew though the calling PG spoke about was for a higher cause, but something in me told me that it wasn't the right moment. I had to deny PG's request.

(I remembered what Guitar had made me promise . . . I was to go slow this time.)

I was glad to see Nadja after my return to Bangalore. I shared my Mumbai experience with her, and she was glad that it had brought a change of view in me.

But the moment I spoke to her about PG and his offer, steams of rage went flying through her, and once again, I found myself unable to understand her . . . All I could hear was her closing statement, 'You are such a waste of talent.'

Later the same day, I received a call from PG who mentioned that the gods of guitar themselves were performing for a charitable event and they wanted to give me another opportunity to share the stage with them for a better and a bigger cause. I agreed to be a part of the charity event which PG had organised.

I looked at my guitar and smiled at her. We shared our thoughts for a while.

She spoke something different that day . . . *She spoke her own mind, just like the days whenever she got angry with me. But this time, her voice had no anger to it, but a warning, screaming in silence.*

After another performance with god themselves, a newfound revelation entered my universe. Time passed by and more and more followers started to knock at my door . . . They wanted more . . .

Media went on covering stories on me and my sporadic appearance on stage. They started creating their own facts to support their delusions. A lot on my life had been circulating around, and I found myself building my own defence wall from these gossips.

I never read those gossips. 'The media wrote what they wanted to write,' I pacified my mind.

Ignoring everything around me, I had been spending a lot of time with Guitar and had lost track of everything in my life . . . Until one fine day I started missing Travel.

I wanted to see new pictures, meet new faces, but I had been caged by my first love.

So, what next?

I called PG and signed up a contract with him. *I thought he was different.*

Life moved back to where it was months ago. PG turned out to be a shrewder businessman than Mr Naren . . . In six months, he had me squeezed dry.

It was only later I got to know that the charity event was just a cover for him to turn his sins into his gold. His heart was always pumping cash instead of blood to his brains.

He was making me forget the picture I was to sketch and insisted I drew a new one for him. I revolted against by turning some of my shows upside down. Hoping crowd would write me off my miseries.

But somehow that too became a message for them, and they took me even higher.

Even if I had nothing to share, the crowd wanted to come and see me . . . Just for the glimpse of me on stage, the crowd went insane.

This time, nothing could help.

Even Nadja's presence did not help me build the picture that I had taken so long to paint in my universe.

The messages that once helped me colour my world suddenly ran dry. The paintings that I had painted before had no connection to its canvas.

Those six months—felt like an eternity and my heart and mind was no longer my own. I had been travelling and performing round the clock, and I had started to hate the very sight of both (Guitar included) The day when I was free from PG, I ran straight to my home . . . And locked myself in my own sweet little universe.

There were no more messages around, but the gossips were flocking the town. News sold dirt cheap and yet they made fortunes at my expense.

Darn, I should not have read those gossips.

Media can be butchers at times . . . Friends? I still have my doubts . . .

But that night I went to sleep at peace again.

(I woke up to an early morning. A brand-new sound of a new beginning; the birds were a happy lot.)

This is not a place where I last went to sleep. There is something about this place that is different? Even though every single piece of furniture, the colour on the wall, the carpet, and every single curtain look the same, something inside me tells me it is not.

I looked around; the medicine cabinet hanging by the wall was left open. I was lying on a bed of whites, and I had been tightly secured to it with straps that heavily pinned me down. I could only move my eyes, and my head had been glued to the pillows—somehow.

They say I have lost my mind and also tell that I am evil and that I talk to the devil. There is nothing I can do to educate the majorities on the truth of reality. I had tried my level best, and they got me labelled immediately.

The price of finding the truth and sharing got me imprisoned to this magnificent place where they say they can treat your mind well until you get back to the reality—what majority believes to be true.

'Stupid of them not to understand, how can they not know?' *Stop talking, I told my curious mind. It would only add more evidence for the majority to brand me with what they have already been labelling me to be.*

There were folks who entered the room, all dressed in their whites. Two gentlemen and two ladies . . . Um! Yes, I am pretty sure . . .

They released me from the bed and took me to a room where a seasoned, matured gentleman entered and started questioning me on my messages. I told him what I knew.

They gave me a surge of energy which took the daylights out of my universe, and I found myself sitting on a chair after moments passed me by.

The chair was slightly inclined, and my head was hanging sideways towards left on its rest. I was unable to move myself, but I could find myself struggling to reach towards my right.

There he was . . . Stephen, my ten-year-old grandson . . . He will be fifty-two by the time he has to deliver my final message . . .

He is the only one who seems to understand what I have always been telling. He is my friend, he knows what I say is truth. Though his parents are also one of the responsible people who got me where I am right now, he has never given up on me.

The silence was gone . . .

Nadja was picking up the broken glasses while she was still sharing her last few thoughts of the moment.

I smiled to her. *She had no clue why I did what I did then. She had never before seen an angry moment of mine.*

I was also equally surprised with myself as nothing seemed to make any sense.

And to add to my epileptic insanity, I went on a senseless journey, and the road was my only guide again—taking me wherever it could take.

This time my curious mind was overpowered by its first cousin, my heart. And my heart took me to Gokarna before I could recollect my sense and understand where it had brought me.

I was happy that I finally had let go of my curious mind and had allowed my heart to guide me through to this beautiful place again. But there was still something void that was left inside me, and it was still pressing the air around. I tried not to bother much and went on my wild exploration with the nature again.

It was then when I met a travelling soul who changed the way my reality would be forever . . .

He introduced himself as Stephen—he went on to share his story, his passion, his interest, and his family. He had my attention while he narrated the story of his life. An interesting character, and I was happy meeting a face that spoke the same language—the language of heart.

After a while, he started talking about the story of his grandfather—*Karl Heidegger, a famous German philosopher and writer of his time. He was a famous artist who wrote plays, books, and poetries in late fifties. It seems he had written several successful books that had been the foundation of many revolutions and transformed the world it was then. However, in his later life, he had been labelled as someone who had been bestowed by evil and was labelled mentally unfit. He had been sent to a mental asylum. Though his behaviour had turned violent, Stephen always knew that his granddad was telling something which others could not understand, and he knew he spoke the truth. He always visited his granddad whenever her got an opportunity and spent time with him when he was a kid. He spoke about how his granddad shared stories with him, the ones that he had written and how it changed the social thoughts; he went on to add that his grandfather was the greatest thinker of all time but highly misunderstood—even by his own.*

Before I could get involved completely with my thoughts, Stephen prodded to check if I was really listening to him. I smiled and gave him the assurance that I was listening to him indeed. He then went on to share something that he mentioned he had not shared with anyone until now. The secret—his grandfather had sworn him to keep by himself, until time was right to be shared.

I inquired why he chose to share the secrets with me which his grandfather had asked him not to share with anyone. He quickly reminded me that he had also mentioned that he should share it when the time was right; and he thought that the time had come, and I was the right person to share the secret.

For a moment I thought he might have been a soulful traveller trying to find his purpose of life and had lost himself to an illusion and was desperately trying to escape from it. *I played along, madness creates madness, and I was game for it. The night was silent and empty, and I was up for a story to get me by the slowly ticking time.*

Stephen continued, 'I had to be here today. You know, I had promised my granddad that in time I would make this trip to India. He told me then that I would be meeting someone here today.'

I gave him a dry laugh and said, 'Maybe it's your destiny you are going to meet today.'

He smiled and ignored my comments and went on with the story about a book which his grandfather had handed over to him. *This was his grandfather's unpublished work and the one he had completed during his final days in the asylum—place where he had to spend the last few days of his life. Stephen mentioned his grandfather never spoke about the book to any other living soul. It was only him, with whom his granddad had confided and had shared a set of instruction to share the message across.*

The moment Stephen mentioned 'Message' a sudden flash ran through my universe.

It was a jolt that reminded me of what I had been after my life. But the messages that I had received so far—it was something that I had been receiving it directly and had been sharing it with the help of my guitar and my songs. What message could he bring this time in a form of a book? Curious mind was already shouting loud.

He handed me a small note book—*it was fairly an old one that had been covered in a leather case to protect it from wear and tear. I opened it and took a quick glance, and honestly, I did not bother to pay much attention to the content inside it at that moment. I guess at that moment I just read the author's name and quickly moved across the pages . . . Nothing went inside my head at that moment.*

Stephen asked me to go through the story and mentioned that I might be interested to know more, and saying this, he bid goodbye. I walked up to him and thankfully returned the book. He insisted that I keep it and read it whenever I felt the moment was right.

Days rolled by and my lazy little soul found itself back in Bangalore. For a few days I did not realise Nadja's absence from the apartment. One fine day, I realised her silence had been longer than usual, and I went to her room—there was no response.

After a moment of waiting, I allowed myself to her room. The room gave an instant impression of no soul living inside I found a note left on top of the study table. I quickly went through it.

It was a goodbye note from Nadja. It wrote:

Kabir, please forgive me for what I have done. The gossip on your life that found its way to the majority was my doing.

My *return to India was to collect information on you and cover as much as gossips that I could to help benefit my career aspiration. I return with memories of good days with you and if I have hurt you in anyway, I am sorry.*

I stood there with the entire canvas in front of me washed clean white and the moments in it frozen.

Those were the last words from Nadja. I never heard from her.

❖

Days had passed since Nadja had left, and I was painting no more pictures in time.

One fine day, while cleaning up my closet, I found the book Stephen had handed over to me. I had completely forgotten about it.

I opened it and started reading it. It had the title 'Gossips of Reality' written on it. I sat there reading hours before the story got over.

I have no explanation to what I had just read . . . Was it a joke? Was it a nightmare? Was it someone's bad idea of joke on me? Thoughts started to flood my mind again . . .

What I had just finished reading was the story of my own life . . .

(It was the same story that you just completed reading.) The only part missing to it . . . the story of Rachel was not included in it.

For a moment I wanted to believe it might have been one of the cheap tricks media played on me to gather more gossip; then my thoughts hastily moved to Nadja. While the thoughts were running havoc inside my universe, my curious mind caught hold of a yellow paper sticking out from the leather cover of the note book. I carefully took the cover out to find a yellow envelope inside. It was sealed and had not been addressed to anyone.

I tore open the envelope and found a letter inside, it read:

Dear Kabir,

If you find yourself reading this letter in time, I thank my stars to have been blessed me with the gift—of seeing the truth.

The truth came to me in form of 'Messages'. I shared those messages with the world through my poetries and plays. At first, majority followed it closely; they took me to a place where they thought I should rightfully need to reside. I thought they understood what I had to share.

I thought they were ready to understand the reality of infinity and started sharing the ultimate truth that I had been lucky to see—they were unable to understand my messages further. They quickly branded me insane; forget the world—my own flesh and blood did that to me.

Stephen, my grandchild, he is the son of my second born, and he is the only one who understands what I have to say. I have given him the responsibility to reach you the last work of mine, the one I wrote only for you.

Your life so far has been a work of my imagination, and when I realised this reality, I wanted to change it forever. I wanted to give you a chance to write your own story—not the story that my imagination has created to cover its own losses in time.

The story of departure and arrival in your life had to be written—the way it was. But with this note, I wanted to ensure that I could leave behind a fresh new canvas for you to create your own reality.

Wish you luck with a new beginning; be careful of your thoughts.

Yours,

Thoughtfully . . .

I remained quiet in my universe for several days. I was unable to think straight. I thought of sharing it with my parents, but I was afraid that they would never understand. *I remembered how Karl had been misunderstood by the majority, and how his own flesh and blood had conspired for his banishment.*

Months had gone after I had read that letter. The whole universe in me was desperate to find the truth of my own reality; I tried every possible way to track down Stephen to find more explanation, if any, his grandfather had shared with him.

However, the Heidegger family had suddenly disappeared after the death of Karl in nineteen sixty-two and had been living a new existence somewhere unknown. Karl's children could not face the majority for what their father had been and chose to live an anonymous life.

If only had I taken a moment to read at least a page when Stephen handed me the book . . . But what can one do when moments have passed away?

After the biggest struggle with my thoughts, the one that I had never before seen in my life, I went on to share what I had to with my parents. As confirmed, they thought my dream had finally got hold of me.

They took me to a shrink for a therapy sessions, I could feel how Karl might have felt when his own flesh and blood doubted him . . . *Betrayed.*

I shared what I had to share with the therapist who had been deeply analysing what I had to say. She concluded, it was a stress-related dysfunction that I was suffering from and ordered to go through a recovery session. This went on for some time. I was being turned into something that I was not; no one wanted to believe what I had to say. *They had their explanations for the story written in the note book—they suggested that the letter was written by me—my unconscious mind had written it for me without my own knowledge.*

(The handwritings did not match with mine, but they say there are studies and artefacts to prove their theory—cases of people suffering from mental disorder, capable of getting such extraordinary jobs done were well documented and timely referred to—as in cases such as mine.)

I knew my struggle to prove my story would take me to a place where Karl had warned me before. I remained silent. The doctors and my parents did what they had to do; I remained with myself closely and did not allow anything to break me down.

A month had passed since my parents and the doctors were doing what they believed was best for my reality, but my mind silently was searching for the answer to the final truth.

I remembered Karl mention about the blank pages left in the notebook . . . I grabbed a pen and wrote . . . *breaking free from the regulars* . . . To a new beginning . . . *Hopefully my own story is written in time for me.*

My phone rang . . . it was . . . Rachel . . .

. . . It is eight in the morning, and it's still dark and empty outside. I peeped through the window and not even a single soul is venturing to the open; the street lights were switched on, and it was lighting up the surrounding trees, which seemed to be gracefully surviving on the artificial life-support system.

This is not a place where I last went to sleep. There is something about this place that is different? Even though every single piece of furniture, the colour on the wall, the carpet, and every single curtain look the same, something inside me tells me it is not.

I can hear a footstep approaching my room; it is my mom—she wants me out of my bed and wants me to finish my early morning chores and get ready for the breakfast. My lazy little soul wants to remain in the warmth of my own little universe and does not want to come out from my bed.

But you know moms—the next I heard was her loud shout 'Kevin, you have exactly three seconds to get up and freshen yourself, before I come there and shape you right . . .'

Where does she get her anger from? . . .

'Peace.'